Broken

An Evergreen Academy Novel

Ruby Vincent

Published by Ruby Vincent, 2019.

Prologue

My feet scrabbled for purchase. The wind was blowing against my back, tugging and pushing me over the side, but its strength wouldn't be enough to carry me if he let go.

I twisted my neck and peered down at the unforgiving drop. This was it. It would all end here.

I guess I knew when I started this that it could only end one way. I wish I could say I would have done things differently, but the truth is, I wouldn't have changed a thing.

I swore they would all know my pain... and after this, I won't know pain at all.

Turning back, I let my eyes flutter shut... and let go.

Chapter One

"He is such a little cutie," Sofia cooed. "It must be hard to be away from him all year."

I glanced up from my list and gazed at my best friend playing with my son. Of course, she didn't know he was my son. No one did.

I smiled at the sight. "You have no idea."

Adam toddled around Sofia's plush ivory carpet picking up, chewing on, and dropping a bunch of the toys she had gotten him. I told her she had gone overboard with the gifts, but she ignored me. She had been radiating excitement over the two of us coming to stay. Between her father's overseas business trips, her mother living at the office, and her nanny being let go; Sofia practically lived in her oversized mansion alone.

She picked up the one-year-old and settled him on her lap. "When does your mom come back from the cruise?"

"Next week." I reached for a textbook and placed it over my papers. "She's having fun. Tipsy every time she calls."

Sofia laughed. "Your mom is so cool. It's too bad she's going to miss your birthday."

"We'll celebrate when she comes back, but I wanted her to have some time off. She's never been on a cruise and the last few years have been... hard for us."

Sofia tried to hold my gaze, but soon lowered her eyes. She didn't know how to handle what I told her at the end of freshman year and I didn't know how to tell her the rest. I felt like all the things that still needed to be said were hanging in the air between us.

"You know if you need anything," she began, "or if there's anything I can do, just tell me."

My fist curled on top of the textbook. "Sofia, you're literally already the best friend anyone could have. I don't know many people who'd let me show up on their doorstep with my baby brother and mooch off them."

"You're not mooching of—"

"Sofi, darling! What is Rudolpho"—the door flung open—"doing here?"

The three of us blinked at the stunning brunette woman that appeared in the doorway and she blinked back at us. I recognized her instantly from the gallery of photos and portraits of her all over the house. This was Madeline Richards—owner of Honey Hair Care and single-handedly responsible for transforming the frizzy split-end mess that was my hair into a shiny chestnut halo.

She was even prettier than the photographs suggested. The smart cashmere sweater and red pants were typical of the bold but classy style she had been cultivating in the media. She had a light dusting of makeup on her heart-shaped face, and of course, her hair was perfect.

"Oh, hello," she said to me. "I don't believe we've met. My name is Madeline Richards."

Sofia heaved a sigh. "She knows who you are, Mom. She's my best friend and she's only been staying with us for the past two weeks."

Madeline looked faintly surprised. "Have you? Oh, dear, you must think me so rude. Forgive me for not introducing myself earlier." Her eyes flicked down to Adam. "And who is this?"

"This is her little brother, Adam—also been staying with us."

"Staying with us?" A slight wrinkle appeared between her brows. "What do you mean?"

"Mother, they've both been here for the summer."

"What? But— We're not equipped to take care of an infant."

"*We* haven't been taking care of an infant," Sofia shot back. "Valentina has."

"But wouldn't he be happier with his mother?"

Yes, he would, I thought.

"Their mom is out of town," replied Sofia. Her nose was wrinkling the way it did when she spoke about—and apparently to—her mother. "They have nowhere to stay, we have room, and you're never here anyway so I didn't think you'd care. And seeing as it took you two weeks to even notice, I was right."

The wrinkle was glaring now. "I do not appreciate your tone, Sofia Lorraine Richards."

Sofia pinked and mumbled an apology under her breath. Madeline nodded. "In the future, you need to discuss things like this with me first. Is that understood?"

She heaved a sigh. "Yes, Mom."

"Which brings me to why I'm here. Why is Rudolpho in my living room? Am I planning an event I don't know about?"

I ducked my head. This one was on me.

"It's Valentina's sixteenth birthday in two days," explained Sofia. "I'm throwing her a party."

What she meant by that was she had called up her mother's designated party planner, Rudolpho, and set him to handling the details.

Madeline gaped at her. "A sweet sixteen in two days? Here? But Rudolpho can't pull off an event that big in such a time."

Event that big?

"No, Mrs. Richards," I said quickly. "It's just going to be the three of us."

She didn't seem to have heard me. "The place is a mess. Also, have you bought a dress yet? And what in the world are we going to do with your hair? Honestly, Sofi, why didn't you tell me sooner?"

Adam crawled out of Sofia's lap and made his way over to her mother.

"I'll have to speak to Rudolpho and— Oh!" Adam balled her red pants in his tiny fists and used them to get to his feet. He stared up at Madeline, waiting.

"You can hold him," I offered. "He likes new people."

"Uh, I shouldn't. This is a new sweater." She bent down and carefully removed Adam from her leg. "Go to your sister, darling. Go on." She made a little shooing motion. "Go. Go."

"Oh, Mom," Sofia groaned, sinking her head into her hands.

"I have to go. Rudolpho and I have details to settle." Madeline backed out of the room and disappeared. Sofia peeked at me through her fingers.

"There you have it, both the reason why I have no siblings and why Mom got me a nanny when I was two weeks old."

I stood to get Adam and place him back on the carpet with his toys. "Should we be worried about this party?" I gave her a look. "Which you don't have to throw me, by the way."

"Um, by the way, I do," she stated, "and we should be cool. Rudolpho knows what we want and he's an expert at holding Mom back. You should have heard what she wanted to do for my sweet sixteen. There was talk of live tigers and fire dancers."

I looked away. "Sorry again about not being there."

"It's okay, Val. I understood."

I knew she did. Her party had been at the beginning of summer before I came. I wanted to go, but the fact that half of our classmates went, killed that idea dead.

"Maybe things will be different this year," she continued. "Jaxson went too far, but he did it in front of the headmaster and the administration. They won't let him get away with it."

I kissed Adam's brown curls rather than answer.

Sofia picked herself up off the carpet. "I should go down there and rescue Rudolpho. I'll distract her with dress ideas. After, let's have lunch by the pool."

"Sounds good."

I shook my head when she left. I couldn't believe this was my life, albeit temporary. Mansions, bathrooms bigger than my entire apartment, housekeepers, party planners, and private chefs that made you pesto pasta with sun-dried tomatoes and then set it out by the Olympic-size swimming pool.

It had been a great summer—giving me plenty of time to think.

I left Adam to play and went back to Sofia's desk. The textbook was shoved off to the side to reveal what I had been truly doing with my summer.

The List

Airi Tanaka

Natalie Bard

Isabella Bruno

Maverick Beaumont
Ezra Lennox
Jaxson Van Zandt
Ryder Shea
The Spades
Evergreen Academy

The names blurred as I tried to read them through again. That was okay, it wasn't as though I needed to. Every name was burned into the fabric of my soul, and there was only one way to remove them.

"Maybe things will be different this year. They won't let him get away with it."

"Things will be different this year," I whispered. The corner of the list crumpled in my hand. "Because *I* won't let him get away with it. Not him or the rest of them."

I PUT ADAM ON MY HIP and left the guest room. Sofia was waiting for me in the dining room with a beaming smile and a cupcake. She wasn't alone. "Happy birthday!"

"Thank you." I accepted her hug.

"Good morning, Valerie," said Madeline. "Happy birthday."

"It's Valentina," Sofia said through gritted teeth. "Mom, shouldn't you have left for work?"

"No, darling." Madeline dabbed the corners of her already perfect mouth and pushed away her breakfast plate. I was a bit late coming down as Adam had recently decided diaper changes were for suckers. "The party is today and we have too much to do. So I want you girls to finish up, and then we're heading out for mani-pedis, dress shopping, getting our hair done—the works."

"Thank you, Mrs. Richards," I said sincerely. "But you don't have to go to all that trouble. We're just having sushi on the terrace."

If anything, Madeline's smile got wider. "This brings me to my next surprise. There will be no sushi; we're going to throw you a proper sweet sixteen party."

"We?" My head swung around to Sofia who gave me a matching incredulous look.

"But Val doesn't want—"

Madeline cut her daughter off. "Every young woman wants a sweet sixteen. Your mother looked after my Sofia last Christmas; the least I can do is give her daughter a proper party. Now hurry and eat your breakfast. We have a nail appointment." Rising from her seat, Madeline gestured at Adam. "I've also called Carmen to come and look after the baby. She'll be here for the rest of your stay."

"But I don't need a—"

Madeline swept out of the room without a backward glance.

"—nanny."

My eyes flicked to Sofia who threw up her hands. "Don't look at me. I warned you about her."

Sighing, we sat down and did what Madame Madeline commanded. We finished up our breakfast and Sofia's former nanny came in halfway through to whisk Adam away.

"I thought you said Rudolpho had my back," I told Sofia as we climbed the stairs.

"He does, but he also has a love of getting paid."

"What am I in for? There won't be tigers or fire dancers, right?"

She grinned. "Only for the fact that she probably couldn't have gotten them late notice... unless she could, of course."

Sofia veered off to her bedroom, leaving me gaping after her.

I showered and dressed quickly and the two of us met Madeline at the door. She peered at me over her sunglasses.

"I love your necklace, darling. I have one just like it. Where did you get yours?"

I placed my hand over the peridot pendant. "I ordered it from a catalog. So," I began when she opened her mouth again. "I'd love to hear more about the party. You said real sweet sixteen, but since it's just the four of us..."

Her tinkling laugh made the rest of my sentence fade in my throat. "It won't be just us. It was very late notice, but I got Rudolpho to dig up Sofi's party list and invite all your friends from school. Nearly everyone said they would come." She clapped. "Isn't that wonderful?"

Madeline didn't wait for an answer. She spun around and glided out the door while I stood rooted to the spot.

All my friends from school...

"I'm so sorry." Sofia grabbed my shoulder. "I'll tell her off, cancel the party, and we'll do what we planned. I promise, I'll fix this."

"No." The word was out before I registered what I was saying. "No, it's fine. She went through so much trouble. It would be rude to cancel."

"Rude? Val, you don't have to worry about hurting my mom's feelings. She'll always have another party to throw." She gave me a little shake. "It's your birthday. You should enjoy it."

I smiled at her. Sofia truly was a good friend, no matter what we went through last year. She thought I didn't want to cancel to be nice. She had no idea.

"It's not me—"

"Girls, what's taking so long?" Madeline called from the front porch.

The two of us picked up our feet and followed her out. It was a perfect morning on the Richards estate. A front lawn of small hills and dips was covered with rose bushes and small gardens. Sofia's home was three stories of bedrooms, bathrooms, a ballroom, bowling alley, two dining rooms, and a sauna. Impressive, and she lived in one of the *smaller* mansions.

Evergreen and its academy sprung up decades ago and as it established itself as the best school in the country, the mega-rich bought up the surrounding properties and made it their mission to get themselves, and their demon seeds, into the school. Almost all of the classmates who tortured me lived in the area or the surrounding towns, they would have no trouble dropping by tonight, but it wasn't me I was worried about.

"Sofia, are you going to be okay?" I asked under my breath. "The last day of school made it clear I'm still marked, and now people are going to figure out we're still friends. They could come after you too."

Sofia lifted her chin. "I don't care. I'm not going to play along like I hate you. You're my best friend; I've got your back."

I put a hand on her arm to stop her from getting into the limo. "Sofia, the things they did to me... I won't let that happen to you."

"I said I don't care. I can take whatever they've got."

I closed the distance between us. "It's not just them," I whispered. "What about the Spades? Walter McMillian?"

Sofia's knuckles were turning white under her tight hold on the hood, but when she spoke her tone was even. "They killed him because he tried to turn the school against the Spades and overthrow the system." She cracked a smile. "You and I aren't planning a revolution."

Don't be so sure of that.

"Besides," she continued. "Mom's outed me. No one would believe we aren't friends now that she's announced we're throwing you a party. So we might as well let her make us over and enjoy part of your birthday."

She slid into the car, and after a pause, I followed. It wouldn't do for Sofia to get caught up in what I had planned this year. This was between me and the Knights.

SOFIA'S RELATIONSHIP with her mother was rocky at best, but I couldn't deny the woman knew how to throw a girls' day. We primped from head to toe, picked up the most gorgeous dresses, then stopped for lunch at the Evergreen Promenade where I had the best soup and salad lunch ever created. Madeline was actually pretty charming when she was present; the only issue was she rarely was.

"I should get back so I can oversee the setup." Madeline perched her mirrored sunglasses on her nose and handed her bags to the driver. We were standing outside the restaurant on the multicolored cobblestones of the shopping center. "Do you girls want to stay a bit longer? I can send the car back to pick you up."

"That'd be great, Mom. Thanks."

"Of course, darling." Madeline kissed the air near Sofia's cheeks before sliding into the car.

I waited until it pulled away from the curb to speak.

"Sofia, we're not friends."

"What?" She goggled at me like I'd slapped her. "What are you talking about?"

"Tonight, at the party," I explained. "You tell everyone we're not friends and you make them believe it. I've been convinced, okay. The Spades are real and the marks are serious. I'm not letting them come after you like they did that Walter guy."

"Val, I told you, I'm not pretending. Besides, what happened to Walter McMillian was awful, but it was also over thirty years ago. Whoever made up the Spades then is long gone from the school."

"And whoever makes them up now is just as vicious," I countered. "Sof, we never found out who made me fall down the stairs."

A flicker of unease showed in her eyes. "Yeah, but—"

"No buts. You told me things get bad when the marked refuse to leave and fight back. Well, I'm planning on doing a hell of a lot of fighting back this year, and if they want me out, they'll have to carry me out."

"Val, don't say things like that!"

I was unmoved. I heard her concern. Understood it. But still it couldn't reach me. "This is why I have to keep you out of it. I *will* make them pay for what they did to me from the Knights, to the Diamonds, to the Spades, and that entire fucking school." Looking her dead in the eye, I stepped closer as hers got bigger. "Sof, I love you, but we're not friends."

Her chin trembled. "I don't think you understand what you're doing..."

"I know exactly what I'm doing." I took her hand. "You have to trust me, and we have to come up with a lie that people will believe." I tried for a smile. "Consider it your birthday present to me."

"I was going to give you dinner from a famous sushi chef and a private show from the Undisturbed," she replied, cheeks red. "Instead, you want me to support a suicide mission. Not an even trade-off."

I gaped at her. "You're getting the Undisturbed? Sofia, that's—"

"Was," she snapped. "Not anymore." Sofia sidestepped me and marched off. Sighing, I ran to catch up to her. "...what Jaxson did to you was awful." Her rant was still going full steam. "What they *all* did to you was awful, but you can't fight them by yourself. And finding out who the Spades are? No one knows who the fuck they are! That's the point!"

"Sofia..." I trailed off. I didn't know the words that would calm my irate best friend which is why I held off on telling her what I was going to do.

"I thought you were feeling better this summer and—"

"And what?" I ran out in front of her and pulled her up short. "Even if I came back pretending nothing happened, they would still be coming after me! Last year, I played nice and wound up with a concussion, broken wrist, dislocated knee, and the whole school finding out that I— That I got a—"

I doubled over, clutching my chest as I gasped. Phantom fingers ran across my body, wrapping around my wrist... and clamping down.

"Val?" I jerked when she touched my shoulder. "Val, I'm sorry."

Taking a deep breath, I calmed my racing heart. "Don't be sorry," I rasped. "It's not your fault." After a while, I straightened. Her eyes were dripping with even more concern than normal but I didn't need that right now. "But I need you to understand that I have to do things differently if I'm going to end this once and for all, and I can't be worried about you the whole time. Walter McMillian tried to protect his friend and was killed; I won't let them hurt you."

Her neck bobbed as she swallowed. "Val, I'm going to say this once—just once. Why don't you drop out of Evergreen? I know you hated your old school, but literally anywhere has to be better than this."

I shook my head. "A diploma from Evergreen and I can send in blank applications to any university in the country, and get in with a full ride. You know where I'm from. Kids in my neighborhood don't bother to dream of getting out. They accept that it's not happening. I have this opportunity, and no one is going to take it away from me. They can't. I have... people depending on me."

She chewed her lip, staring at me for a long time, then she nodded. "Okay. I get it."

"Thank you."

She linked her arm through mine and we kept walking. "But I want to help. Tell me what to do."

"First, we have to make people believe that we're not friends. Then we have to find out more about the Spades."

"That's going to be hard. We don't know who or where to start."

"Yes, we do," I stated as a memory formed in my mind in crystal clear picture. "Last year, Halloween night. The masquerade ball. We find the person who started all of this."

"YOU LOOK LOVELY."

I lifted my gaze and caught her smile in the mirror. I might have offered one back, but smiles didn't come as easily these days. "Thanks, Carmen."

Although, I would have given more credit to the dress than me. It was a stunning, tea-length emerald green gown that Madeline had taken one look at, said matched my eyes perfectly, then told the attendant we were buying it before I even had a chance to look at it properly. Unsurprisingly, her taste was spot on.

"And thank you for taking care of Adam," I added. The baby snoozed on her shoulder with no care to her being a perfect stranger. "I hope he wasn't too much trouble today."

Sofia's former nanny was much younger than I was expecting. Apparently, she had started working for the family when she was nineteen, but it was still hard to buy that she was in her thirties.

"This one could never be trouble."

I stifled a snort. She didn't know Adam during his teething phase.

"I was happy to help," she continued. She crossed the room and carefully placed the baby in his bassinet. "I haven't seen my Sofia in months. They shouldn't lock you up in that academy like that. That's just too long to go without seeing my favorite girl."

Carmen came over to my side and reached for the emerald necklace on the nightstand. I lowered my arms so she could put it on. "At least your birthday is during the summer so you've been able to have a real party. The best part is all of your friends can still be here."

I tensed. Having my birthday outside of Evergreen was a plus, until Madeline brought all my *friends* to me. I had no idea how tonight was going to go, but I did know one thing...

I met my reflection's eyes. In another life, they might have scared me. The sharp, glittering coldness was something that was always held in *his* eyes, and being anything like that monster was reason to worry. But not now.

"Thanks again," I said after she hooked the clasp. "He should sleep through the night, but if not, come and get me."

"No, no, no. You're his sister, not his mother. The only thing you need to do tonight is have fun."

Now I smiled. "Oh, I'm going to have fun tonight. Mark my words."

I put on the final touches and then left our room. A thumping reverberated through the mansion, beckoning me outside to the party. It had started half an hour ago, but I decided to be fashionably late.

A lot could be said about Madeline Richards, but none of it could be that she didn't know how to throw a party. She told me they had gone with a jewel theme and I had no clue what that was supposed to look like, then I stepped onto the veranda.

My mouth fell open.

Emerald and silver had become the official colors and they graced the shimmering tablecloths topped by crystal centerpieces. Lights had been strung up along the massive backyard with bulbs in the shape of diamonds. As for the guests, there were no polos or jeans in sight. Girls in jewel colors, and guys in suits that probably equaled the cost of a handful of jewels.

This was amazing. The sweet sixteen a girl always dreams of... if it wasn't for the hostile eyes that fell on me the moment I stepped out.

"My mom forced me to come since she does business with Madeline." I turned my head and spotted Penelope and Lola. Summer had been good to them. Both girls were sporting new haircuts and fresh tans. Penelope spoke to her friend, but looked right at me as she said, "I told her I didn't want to party with a diseased slut, but she said I have to play nice for at least an hour."

My eyes slid away from them and I made to step off the veranda.

"Don't run off, birthday girl." I heard footsteps gaining on me and then a hand fisted in my dress. "Did you ever take care of those STDs? Just want to make sure it's safe to touch things."

I spoke without turning around. "Penelope, you remember I said I'd knock out all those bleached teeth if you didn't stop running your mouth? I think the real question is do you feel safe touching me?"

Suddenly the hand on my dress was gone, and I took off without another word.

"Disgusting bitch!"

I kept moving. The party had been set up in a kind of rectangle. The food table was on one end, a stage was on the other, on the sides were small stand-up tables for people to eat. In the middle was the dance floor, but there weren't many people on it.

I looked around and spotted Sofia standing at a table with Eric, Paisley, and a guy that was either Paisley's boyfriend or Eric's. I didn't know these things anymore since after apologies and promises never to hurt me again, my old friends went right back to tormenting me when Jaxson called the fake truce off. Eric had been the first one to upload the video of me running off stage when the whole class found out I had chlamydia.

I grabbed a plate off the table and dropped random nibbles on it as I drifted closer to their table.

"...insane," I heard Eric say. "Why didn't you tell me Moon was staying here? Is that why you kept dodging me when I asked to come over?"

"What was I supposed to do?" Sofia asked. "I knew you'd flip shit and go on about obeying the Knights and not messing with tradition."

"Of course, I would have," he hissed. "Are you trying to get marked too?"

"No, Eric, which is why I didn't go broadcasting it. Isn't that obvious?" Sofia was all bubbles and sunshine on a regular day so it made it weird to hear her "rich bitch" voice. She had one, and she knew how to use it, but it made me tense just remembering those months when I had been on the receiving end of it. "We were friends before she got marked, and when her mom left for vacation, she asked mine if she could stay. I had no idea she was coming until Madame Madeline announced my 'surprise' at breakfast."

I popped a smoked salmon hors d'oeuvre in my mouth and listened closely. *Please believe her. Please believe her.*

Paisley scoffed. "I swear your mom is so freaking clueless about your life."

"Tell me about it."

"You just better hope the Knights don't think you're still friends." There was an edge of hesitation in Eric's voice that I didn't like.

"Trust me, we're not friends. The girl stays locked up in her room all day and I go about my life. Mom threw her this party because she felt bad for her mom ditching her on her birthday. It's not a big deal."

I shoved a mini empanada in my mouth. She was doing good. She would get them to believe her. I turned away—

—and smacked right into a hard body.

"Damn, girl. That's some dress."

The breath whooshed out of my lungs with the force of a sucker punch. I stumbled away and smacked my thigh into the table. Jaxson Van Zandt grinned into my wincing face.

"It's been way too long, Val." His eyes swept my body. "You look great. Did you miss me?"

I planted my hand on the table to steady myself and my fingers brushed against cool metal. I looked down. Resting beneath my fingertips was a carving knife.

My heart picked up speed as I glimpsed my reflection in the polished surface. I slowly drew the knife to me and wrapped my palm around the handle.

"Because I missed you."

Jaxson's voice brought me crashing back to reality. Shaking myself, I tried to cool the hot spike of rage swarming through me as I released the blade. "I missed you"—I looked him in the eye—"like I miss the chlamydia."

Jaxson lifted a brow. "Ouch."

"What the fuck are you doing here?" I lurched forward, getting right in his face. "Are you out of your mind? Why would you come to my party?"

The smile hadn't left his face and it only served to piss me off more. I never understood this guy. What kind of asshole reveals your medical history to an auditorium full of people, then asks if you've missed him? Everything is a big joke to him.

It only made it worse that he looked so incredible. The start of freshman year had seen him with a buzz cut, but now his golden hair fell to the tips of his ears, and the five studs he now had adorning each one. His blue eyes glittered in the diamond lights, drawing me to them even though I kept trying to look away. Although looking at his eyes was better than following the trail down his open shirt to his exposed chest. Jaxson had worn a suit, but the tie and belt were nowhere to be seen. He wore the overall can't-give-a-shit attitude as well as he wore everything else.

I never denied that he was handsome. They all were. But there was malice like most have never seen behind each one of their eyes.

I swallowed as another thought came to me. "Are the *rest* of you coming?"

To my relief, he shook his head. "Ricky doesn't like parties. Ezra has some boring awards dinner to go to with his mom, and Ryder hates you," he stated bluntly. "But you know that."

I placed my hand to my throat. Yeah, I knew that.

"So it's just you and me tonight." Jaxson reached up and swept a lock of hair behind my ear. Goose bumps erupted all over my body. "I like the new hair."

The new hair was a short bob that barely reached my shoulders. My long chestnut curls had disappeared after Jaxson delivered the final blow.

I smacked his hand away. "I asked you what you were doing here?"

"Calm down, mama. I'm not here to mess with you—"

"I've heard that before."

"—I'm here with the band," he went on. "When they leave, I leave."

"Or you could skip to the part where you leave now."

He chuckled, completely unfazed by my anger. "You know, I really did miss you. Things got heated at the end of the year, but I did what I had to do to make you leave." He sighed. "But clearly it didn't work."

"I told you there was nothing you guys could throw at me that would make me drop out. You'll have to do better than that."

Jaxson cocked his head. "Better than telling the whole school you lied about being a virgin and actually fucked your way to an STD? Better than getting the whole thing on a hundred cameras and making you the trending video on YouTube? That wasn't good enough for you?" He whistled. "Shit, baby. I'm starting to think you like punishment."

My nails dug half-moons into my palms; I clenched my fists so tight. The pressure was building in my body. Anymore and I would burst.

"I'm not your baby," I spat.

"Want to know why I waited and let you have a few weeks of peace?" Jaxson closed the scant amount of distance between us. We were so close the tip of my nose brushed his chin. "People in the music business know that timing is everything. Ride the right moment, and you can take someone from nobody to sensation with one show.

"I could have revealed what I found in your records from the beginning, but then it wouldn't have been in front of the whole class with all their phones out, and you all unsuspecting and trusting because we gave you a little time off." He laughed. "And they think I'm the stupid one."

I didn't speak. Standing there, jaw clenched, I did everything I could to not bury my fist in his face.

Taking a deep breath, I let it out slowly until I trusted myself to speak. "So you lied too," I whispered. "You said you didn't want to do the things you guys did to me, but you put a lot of thought into hurting me for that to be true."

Jaxson's smile dimmed.

"You know I thought you liked me... before everything happened." I lowered my eyes. "My friends would tell me I should take you into the stairwell and get your pants off."

His tongue darted out, swiping across his lips. "Why didn't you?" he breathed.

I shook my head. "I wasn't ready to be with anyone then, but still I thought one day, I would be ready for you."

I lifted my hand and tangled a finger in his hair. Jaxson peered at me through hooded eyes. His breathing picked up speed, almost as fast as my racing heart.

"But it was all a trick." I ran my fingers along his scalp, making his eyes flutter shut. "You never liked me. Never wanted me as badly as I wanted you."

"That's not true." His voice was so soft I barely heard him over the music. A hand snaked around my waist and pulled me as close as two people could possibly be.

I shook my head. "You can't trick me again. I know I was a bet. I know you enjoyed humiliating me in front of the school."

"I did what I had to do." Jaxson pressed his lips to my forehead. "You don't belong at Evergreen." He kissed between my brows next. Then the bridge of my nose. He was leaving a burning trail along my face that was cracking my resolve. It was with mixed feelings that I remembered the kisses I shared with Ezra, Maverick, and even Ryder, but I've never kissed Jaxson.

"You have to drop out." His warm breath ghosted over the tip of my nose before he kissed that too. "And believe it or not, I was being kind. There are much worse things that can, and have, been done to get rid of the marked." Jaxson kissed the small space between my nose and lip. There was only one place left for him to go. "Don't let it get that far. Transfer out, Val. End this."

Jaxson brought his lips down on mine. I twisted at the last second and he caught my cheek.

"I will end this," I said. I rose up and put my mouth to his ear. "I'm coming back and I'm going to make every single one of you pay. No mercy, just like you showed me." Jaxson stiffened in my hold. "You're going to regret the day you sat down next to me in homeroom, *baby.*"

I slipped out of his arm and walked off. I felt the eyes on me as I strode across the lawn; I imagined his were boring into me fiercest of all.

Good. I hope he spreads it to his friends too.

"Hello? Hell—" Speaker feedback cut through the party, deafening everyone nearby. Madeline fluttered. "Oh, dear. Excuse me."

Sofia's mom looked even more glamorous than me, but in her case, I figured it was effortless. Her hair was pulled back into a tight bun and the ruby-red wraparound gown fit her like a glove. She caught my eye and beamed at me from the stage. "I hope everyone is having a good time," she said into the mic. "Now, before we kick things off, let's have a round of applause for the birthday girl."

A weak smattering of clapping followed that but Madeline didn't let it get her down. "Valentina is a special girl who deserves every happiness in life and it is my pleasure to celebrate her sixteenth birthday with her. It is also my pleasure to announce her favorite band..."

My eyes widened. *Wait, no. It can't be.*

"The Undisturbed!"

I thought I was done with the open-mouthed gaping, but apparently, I had one more in me as the members of my favorite band jogged out onto the stage. The cheers that went up this time were ear-splitting, and I twisted around to look for Sofia.

I thought she canceled them. How are they here? How are they seriously here?!

"Thank you, everyone," said lead singer, Dougie. "It is an honor to be here tonight for Valentina. Where is she? Let's get her up on stage."

Dougie was getting closer and closer. I looked down. My feet were carrying me up all on their own. That was good because my brain went offline five seconds ago.

The dance floor went from empty to packed in a heartbeat. Everyone rushed the stage as I climbed up the steps and placed my hand in Dougie's. His bearded cheeks stretched into a smile.

"This is for you, Valentina."

"I'm here with the band. When they leave, I leave."

It was easy to forget that Jaxson was the son of a legendary music producer, which was funny because he didn't like to let people forget it. I wish I could say as I looked into the eyes of my celebrity crush that I started to hate him less, but this didn't change a thing.

Dougie started crooning one of my favorite songs and I let the music take over. I danced unheeding of the people watching me or the knowledge of what this year would bring. At that moment, I was just a girl at her sweet sixteen.

The band let me stay on stage through the whole set. My night couldn't have gotten any more amazing.

"Now we have one more song we'd like to sing to the birthday girl, and I think you all know this one so feel free to join in."

The guitarist started playing the tune to "Happy Birthday" and I looked over the sea of bodies to see the sliding doors open. Sofia wheeled out a cart loaded down with a massive, five-layer birthday cake—green of course.

I climbed off the stage as the crowd parted to make way for her. My favorite band at my back, my hated classmates on my sides, and Sofia beaming at me as she turned the cart and set it in front of me. None of this was what I planned for my birthday, but I guess it could have been worse.

Sofia smiled at me as I reached for the cake knife. “Happy birthday”—her expression morphed in a blink—“bitch.”

Sofia yanked and the cart tilted to the side. I screamed as a mountain of frosting, fondant, and chocolate batter crashed on top of me.

Chapter Two

"I'm sorry. I'm sorry. I'm so sorry."

I peeked out through the hole in the towel and gave her a look. "Sof, stop apologizing. You only did what I told you to do."

Sofia sank onto the sheets looking wretched. She was still dressed in her party gown, even though everyone had been sent home hours ago. I had only just gotten out of the shower. It's harder than I thought to get icing out of your hair.

"I shouldn't have gone along with it," she moaned. "I ruined your birthday."

I pulled my robe tighter and sat down next to her. "I got to dance onstage with the Undisturbed. You could have lit me on fire and it wouldn't have ruined this night." I bumped her shoulder. "Besides, I should be saying sorry to you. I heard Madeline chewing you out."

She scoffed. "She even grounded me. Can you believe that? Look who decided to act like a parent."

"Bright side: no one will think we're friends now."

She gave me a sad smile. "There is no bright side to this. I really don't like this, Val. I'm... scared."

"Don't be. I promise everything will be okay. I have a plan."

"Will you let me in on the plan?"

"The less you know, the better."

"Sounds like something people say before they kill someone."

I let the towel fall back over my head, blocking my face.

"If you're sure about this... I'll trust you."

"I'm sure." I tossed the towel over my shoulder and stood. Crossing the room, I peeked at Adam and found he was still fast asleep. I stroked his soft little cheek. "I'm going to make everything right."

"Okay. Good night, Val."

"Night."

"DID YOU HAVE FUN WITH Sofia?"

"It was great, Mom." I took my eyes off the mansion fading in my rearview mirror and focused on her. The rest of our vacation had been great even with Sofia being grounded. That didn't look much different since Madeline went back to work and wasn't around to keep her in. "I've got to show you the pictures of the sweet sixteen they threw me."

"That was nice of them." Mom pulled out of the driveway and set us on the lane that led home. "I'll show you mine too. I'm sorry I missed your birthday, baby, but we'll celebrate tonight."

"I know we will, and I'm glad you had fun. You could use a break."

"Not from my Adam." She grinned at him in the rearview mirror. "He's such a good baby. *You* destroyed my figure, gnawed my nipples half off, and screamed whenever I closed my eyes. I started taking it personal after a while."

"Love you too, Mom," I mumbled under my breath.

She cackled. "Let's have dinner at our favorite spot, swing by the mall, see a movie, and pick out a present. Sound good?"

"Perfect."

I was wrong that celebrating my birthday couldn't get any better than being up on that stage. We had so much fun talking about Olivia's cruise adventures and the things Sofia and I got up to that I had no trouble finding my smiles that night.

We stepped into the elevator and Mom pushed the button for the top floor. "Oh, yeah. I've got all your deliveries stacked up in my living room. What's with that? I don't remember you needing all of that for last year."

"It's sophomore year, Mom. Things are even more intense."

"But what is it?"

"Just some books. Things for my new dorm. Stuff like that."

"Okay, but I need you to move them to your room."

"I will."

We stepped off the elevator and went into our apartment. I didn't waste a second in moving the packages into my room. I'd have rather not sent it to the apartment, but sending it to school was out of the question. I couldn't tell Mom what was really in these boxes, but I hadn't lied completely. Sophomore year would be intense, and all these things would ensure I survived it... and they didn't.

I set my list of names on the floor as I checked everything over and packed it away. Second year, first semester; here I come.

SUMMER ENDED MUCH TOO quickly and soon I was piling my things into the car and putting Wakefield in my rearview mirror. I was chatty when we started the two-hour drive, but as the gates loomed closer, I got quieter. I wanted to be here. I had gone through so much to earn my spot at this school, but the girl who rode up to those wrought-iron fences a year ago wasn't here any-more.

"Want me to help you unpack?"

"No, that's okay. It's a long drive. You guys should head back."

"Alright, kid. I'll see you soon then."

Mom joined the line of cars and pulled up to the curb. Like before, there were gray-uniformed staff who sprang into action the moment she popped the trunk. I kissed Olivia, and then climbed over the passenger seat to kiss Adam too.

"I'll miss you, son," I said softly. Adam blinked up at me with huge eyes. "Be good for Grandma."

Whack!

"Ow!" My hand flew to my backside.

"What did you just call me? You watch your language around the baby."

Grumbling, I pulled back and hopped out. Mom beeped before throwing the car in drive and riding off—leaving me alone.

I spun around and faced the gates of Evergreen Academy.

Time to burn this motherfucker to the ground.

I PUSHED INTO MY NEW dorm room and stepped aside so the men could bring in my suitcases, I tried not to be impressed, but I wasn't fooling anyone. This room was bigger than my freshman dorm, and that place had been bigger than our apartment.

My bed was bigger. My desk was bigger. My wardrobe took up almost an entire wall. There was a cute study nook with shelves above for my textbooks.

Gotta give them this much; they hire great interior decorators.

"Thank you," I said to the staff members. They tipped their caps at me and filed out.

I let the door slam shut and then flung myself on the bed. My phone was out and my fingers typing moments after the comforter claimed me.

Me: They put me on the first floor. Rm 105. Where r u?

Sofia: Third floor. Rm 316. They probably want to make sure you don't fall down any more stairs.

Me: Good call.

Sofia: I know you said you had a plan, but I'm glad you'll have Noemi watching your back.

Me: Actually, I won't. No bodyguard for me this year.

Sofia: WHY?!

Me: It's all a part of the plan, Sof. Don't freak. What wasn't a part of the plan was it being harder for us to sneak into each other's rooms. Someone might see us if we try now.

Sofia: I know. This sucks. We'll have to meet up in our secret spot from now on. Unless Rossman goes back to bending Panzer over the couch up there.

I hit her with a wave of vomit emojis.

Me: Thanks for the image! Gross. Why is that our secret spot again?

Her reply was a bunch of LOLs.

I tossed my phone on the pillow beside me and heaved myself up. I was here now. It was time to put things in motion. I went through and unpacked all my stuff, hanging up my clothes, setting out my makeup, then sliding one locked suitcase under my bed. I hoped the security system would protect me from another break-in, but I wasn't taking chances.

When everything was put away, I reached for my phone again.

Me: Did you find them?

I waited with bated breath, counting the seconds *tick, tick, ticking* from the clock as I stared at my phone.

S: Yes. I will send you the information.

Me: Great. Thank you.

I went to set my phone down when a buzz vibrated my hand.

S: Your account is low. I will deposit more money.

I thought about saying no. My fingers were poised to type it, but at the last second, I stopped myself.

More money would come in handy this year.

I pulled up the reply and typed in six letters.

Thanks.

The next text was the information I had asked for.

I stayed up well into the night setting my plans into motion, which is why I didn't welcome the banging on my door early the next morning.

I poked my head out from under my pillow. "Who is it?!"

It was Sunday. Classes didn't start until the next day and Sofia wouldn't be banging on my door begging to get caught. Who was out there and what could they possibly want from me?

"Valentina, it's me."

My irritation melted away. Slowly, I pushed off the covers and padded to the door. Noemi beamed at me over the threshold.

"Hey, Val. How was your summer?"

"Good."

"Did you go anywhere fun?"

"No."

She nodded. "Let me guess, it was homework, homework, homework. You study like crazy, but I tell you, I got through so many books while I was sitting with you in the library that I made my husband jealous. The kids make sure we don't have time to shower, let alone read." She laughed at her joke.

"Bummer."

Noemi clapped. "So, the new semester starts tomorrow which means I'll be outside your door bright and early. After the awards ceremony... the headmaster felt it best I continue to escort you."

"No."

"So I was thinking we..." Noemi trailed off, the smile slipping off her face. "What?"

"No, I don't want an escort this year."

"But, Val, last year you went through—"

"I don't need you to tell me what happened last year." I tried to keep my tone even. "I don't want a bodyguard and I'll tell the headmaster that and sign whatever he puts in front of me."

Her eyelashes fluttered as she blinked at me. "If that's what you want—"

"It is." I stepped back inside and grabbed the door. "Wait here while I change. We can go right now."

I closed the door on Noemi's screwed-up face and got dressed. I stepped out ten minutes later. Noemi fell in beside me, silent as we walked out into the quad.

It was the chaos you'd expect of the final move-in day out here. People ran around meeting up with friends, herding parents, and lugging oversized suitcases. Noemi and I weaved through the chaos without saying a word, but every now and then I caught her looking at me out of the corner of my eye.

Stepping through into administration was night and day what was happening outside. It was deathly quiet in here. Mrs. Khan sat behind reception shuffling papers around while the other office workers had their eyes glued to their computers. You'd think they'd have a lot to do getting ready for a new school year. Looking at them I remembered something Paisley told me.

"There may be a whole administration office with little worker bees banging away at their computers, but Jaxson and the other Knights are the ones who really run this school—at least in the ways that matter."

It was hard to argue with that.

"Mrs. Khan. We need to speak to the headmaster."

She pointed without looking up. "You can go right through."

Headmaster Evergreen wasn't as old as his sallow skin and white hairs suggested. According to Sofia, the man was only in his early fifties, but had been running the school since he took over for his father when he was thirty.

I peered at him through hooded eyes as he gestured for me to take a seat. Evergreen once said he had no idea what it meant to be marked. I believe that like I believe deep down Ryder Shea was really a nice guy.

"What can I do for you, Miss Moon?"

"I won't be needing a bodyguard this year. I'm supposed to sign something for that, right?"

Evergreen's forehead wrinkled with his frown. "You expressed concern last year for your safety and seemed quite pleased with this solution. I must say I'm surprised to hear this after the incident at the awards ceremony."

I gritted my teeth. "Speaking of the ceremony, what did you do about Jaxson Van Zandt stealing my medical records and announcing my business to the school? Last I checked, that was a crime."

Evergreen's face smoothed out. "It was negligence to the highest degree, and I assure you, we take that very seriously. Dr. Miller was let go and new systems have been put in place to ensure this doesn't happen again. Every video of the incident that was put online has been taken down, and our lawyers will ensure no more are posted."

I waited for him to say more. "And?" I pressed when he didn't go on. "How was *Jaxson* punished?"

"Mr. Van Zandt's parents were informed of his actions and he will no longer MC school events."

"That's it? You made me pick up trash for weeks because I broke a television, but Jaxson breaks the law and nothing."

Now his expression changed. Evergreen's frown said everything about how far I would get pushing this. "The punishments I give are not for you to question, Miss Moon. Now let's return to the matter at hand. Why are you refusing an escort?"

I folded my arms. "It's simple. No matter how I look at it... your escort was involved in me falling down the stairs."

The reaction to my accusation was immediate.

"Miss Moon!"

"Excuse me?!"

I sat stony-faced while they raged around me. All I've done over the last few weeks was think about what was done to me, and this was the only thing that made sense.

"That is a serious allegation," Evergreen said. "Do you have any proof of this?"

"Of course there's no proof," said Noemi. "I had nothing to do with it. It was an accident."

"It wasn't an accident." I announced. "I asked the custodians and they said they had no reports of the elevator being broken down that day. Someone put up that sign to make me take the stairs, and then trip over a line that was gone when I came back."

"What line?" Evergreen sputtered. "How can you be sure it was there? And—"

"I know what I felt, Headmaster," I cut in calmly. "But the real problem is... where was Noemi? She was supposed to be standing outside my room waiting for me but she wasn't there when I came out, and she wasn't the one who found me knocked out on the stairs. Some random freshman came back from class and screamed the place down thinking I was dead. That was an hour and a half after she was supposed to meet me."

I turned to Noemi. The woman didn't meet my gaze, her eyes fixed on a point above Evergreen's head. "Why weren't you there? And when you couldn't find me, why didn't you look?"

Noemi still didn't look at me. "I did nothing—"

My hands clamped down on the arms of the chair. "Stop lying!" My anger came up hot and fast. I had liked Noemi. I thought she was my friend. Realizing she must have betrayed me was the final nail in the coffin. "If one more lie comes out of your mouth, the next person I speak to will be the cops. Let's see how many books you read in prison."

Evergreen rose from his seat. "Miss Moon, it won't be necessary to involve the police. I will handle this matter personally."

Noemi fixed on him; her face stricken. "Headmaster, I swear I was not involved in any plot to harm her. I—"

He held up a hand. "We have yet to determine that there was a plot, or even that it wasn't an accident like Miss Moon believes. That will be looked into. But a fact that does remain is you were not at your post at the time of her fall. That is unacceptable."

"But, sir, I—"

Evergreen wasn't letting her get a word in. "Mrs. Kennedy, you no longer work for Evergreen Academy. Please, pack up your things. Security will escort you from the building within the hour."

"But, sir!"

"Headmaster!"

This time the shouts came from both of us. I lurched out of my seat. "Headmaster, you can't get rid of her until I find out who put her up to it." I spun around. "Tell me who it was. Tell me *why*. Did someone pay you?"

Noemi turned her face, hiding her shadowed expression.

"Tell me!" I darted in front of her, trying to make her look me in the eyes. "Was it one of the Knights? The Diamonds?"

"Miss Moon."

Grabbing her arm, I cried, "Was it the Spades?"

"Miss Moon!" roared Evergreen, causing me to jump. "I told you that I will handle this matter. Leave now."

"But, sir—"

"Another but will see you in detention for the rest of the semester. Leave my office."

I bit my lip to stop myself from arguing. Picking up more trash around school wouldn't get me any closer to finding the Spades, and with Noemi falling mute, neither would she.

I let go of her hand and left without another word.

I knew this wouldn't be easy. I also knew it would be dangerous. But I would not stop until I exposed every last one of them.

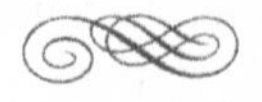

I PICKED UP A NECKLACE, held it to my throat, and grimaced. Sofia was right about one thing: no one looked good in yellow. I honestly don't know what they were thinking making it the sophomore color.

I tried another necklace and tossed that back too. Between the yellow blazer, white button-up shirt, and black-and-yellow plaid skirt; I looked like a preppy banana.

Sighing, I gave up on accessorizing and moved on to the important part of my outfit. I lifted the button camera from the box and carefully put it into place.

Wow. I stepped back and checked myself out in the vanity. *Can't tell the difference at all.*

The tiny camera blended in perfectly among my other buttons. I picked up my phone and fiddled with it until a video of my reflection appeared on the screen. Something so small could see and hear everything I can.

Perfect.

I took the second cam out of the suitcase and tucked it and my phone away in my backpack, then shoved in a change of clothes. I was ready for my first day.

I stepped out of my room into an empty hallway. That was on purpose. I wanted to give everyone a head start to cut down on the harassment I would get on the way to class. That sort of worked.

"Oh, shit. Who let her back in?"

It started the moment I stepped out into the quad. The freshman dorms were right next to the main building, but unfortunately for me, my new dorm was in the back behind the sports complex. It was a long walk to class.

"We shouldn't have to go to school with a diseased slut. What if we catch something?"

"Isn't the first rule of tricking to bag it up? If you're going to be a slut, at least don't be a stupid slut."

"I saw you on YouTube." This came from a girl in a blue uniform—a freshman. "You looked so pathetic running off the stage to cry." The girl trailed me, nipping at my heels. "If you're going to give it out that easily, you should at least be able to take it."

I didn't bother to turn around. All of these people were mindless gnats—annoying, but harmless. I needed to focus all my attention on those that would be harder to take down.

Stepping into the main building, I shut the door on all the vicious taunts and turned for the stairs. Second year meant second floor and this would be my first time setting foot up there. I topped the first landing when I heard their voices.

"—believe she came back."

"The girl's a masochist. She probably has her customers beat her with whips and spank her ass until she's red. She gets off on punishment."

I stiffened at the chorus of laughter that echoed through the stairwell. I knew that voice. Natalie Bard couldn't be mistaken.

"Masochist or not," Airi Tanaka replied, "she's tough. She will not leave and I'm up for first chair this year now that Indira Reddy graduated. Can't we leave it to everyone else to drive our tasty friend out?"

I held still as silence descended.

"Seriously, Airi." Isabella was a cold witch normally so it was saying something to think that her voice had never sounded frostier. "You think we don't all have shit to do?"

"I— I only meant—"

"Cade has to make valedictorian again. Natalie has a tournament coming up to defend her title as grand master. And Mother is pulling me out of school every weekend to practice for the Nutcracker audition. Getting Clara in a Broadway production will pretty much cement my future as principal."

"I k-know. I—"

"No one *wants* to waste their time with Valentina Moon, but the Spades don't take it any easier on the people who cut the marked slack. Would you rather be fucking with her or have them fucking with you?"

"First one. Definitely." I had never heard Airi sound so small. "I was just kidding, Bella."

I heard a sniff. "Whatever. Look, we're about to be late for homeroom. We'll have to corner her afterward."

I let out a breath as I heard them file out. That was until the door slam was immediately followed by the bell.

I hoofed it the rest of the way, bursting through the doors and tearing off for Professor Wheeldon's homeroom class.

The second floor of the academy was almost identical to the first. The same black-and-white marble floors. Heavy drapes covered the large windows and made the space darker than it needed to be. I once thought it made it look romantic.

I skidded to a stop in front of the door. Taking a minute to collect myself, I placed my hand over the button cam to make sure it was in place.

Okay. I'm ready.

I stepped through into the homeroom, and every eye snapped to me. I looked around for a free desk until my gaze met his... and his... and his.

I stopped dead. Jaxson Van Zandt, Ezra Lennox, and Maverick Beaumont gazed at me from the row they claimed at the back of the room. In the row directly in front of them, was Natalie, Airi, and Isabella Bruno.

Only thing needed to complete this hellish picture is—

A whoosh of air tickled my skirt, and I knew before I turned around who it was.

"I had hoped Jaxson was lying..."

I spun to face him.

"...but you actually were stupid enough to come back."

A smile spread across my lips. "I'm sure he told you why, too."

Ryder Shea smirked at me. Silver eyes looked me up and down in the same way I was sizing him up. I was wrong about no one looking good in yellow. It seemed Ryder's special brand of devilishly handsome couldn't be tamed by anything from hideous uniforms to the glint that lit in his otherwise cold eyes whenever he saw me. It was a glint I knew by now came before he dealt his next blow.

"Yes, he did." He cocked his head. "You plan on taking us all down one by one. By yourself. No help. And everyone against you."

"That's right," I said cheerily. "And the best part is"—I leaned in and lowered my voice—"I'm saving you for last. I've got something very special for you."

Ryder's eyes narrowed. "You really are a fucking idiot. There isn't a single thing you can do against me. There is nothing you can do to stop me." He lowered his voice too. "I could choke you in front of the entire school and no one would do a thing."

Anger roiled in the pit of my stomach, boiling inside of me until it was everything I could do not to lunge. *Be smart, Val. Use this anger to take him down.*

"You're wrong," I said after a minute. "You have no idea the things I can do to you, but you'll find out before the year is over."

"You think I'm afraid of you?"

"No, you're not afraid of me." Words Ryder said to me only last year sprang to my lips. "But you should be."

"Excuse me?" A clearly irritated voice broke through our bubble. I peered over my shoulder at Professor Wheeldon. "Are we interrupting?"

"Yes," Ryder snapped.

If possible, Wheeldon turned redder. "Just who do you think you're—! Sit down now!"

I didn't need to be told twice. I turned my back on Ryder and took up a free desk in the middle of the room. I watched Ryder as he strolled past to the back with the rest of the Knights. It was actually a good thing to have them all in one place. They would get a front row seat as I tore every one of them down.

"Hey, Val." Lola spun around in her seat and shot me a grin. "I had a great time at your party. Especially that bit at the end."

A few people around us snickered.

"Half the class missed it," she continued, "so I made sure to put up the video of you getting caked so everyone could see."

No one tried to smother their laughter now.

"Quiet!" Professor Wheeldon heaved himself out of his chair and stared us all down. He was a big man—like bodybuilder big. His suit was neatly pressed and a stylish pair of glasses perched on his nose, but I couldn't shake the impression this guy would look more at home in a gym.

"Thank you," he began. He stepped in front of his desk and leaned against it. "Announcements will begin in a moment, so before they do, I would like to introduce myself. This will be my first year at Evergreen. I'm taking over for the former English II professor."

Whispers broke out around me and my brows snapped together. Was a new teacher really that big of a deal?

"Rules for homeroom are as follows: No talking. No eating. No fighting. You will come in, work, and then you will leave. Is that understood?"

He got a resounding yes from the class.

"Good. Then first things first. Your seating assignments."

Cue the groans. I might have groaned too if I thought it would do any good. Grudgingly, I got out of my seat when he called my name and moved to the third from the last row. Down the names he went until I learned exactly why having a new teacher was a bad thing.

Even though the staff wouldn't admit it, I knew the entire school was aware I was marked. I would have thought an old teacher would have known not to sit me next to Maverick and Ezra, but sadly this guy was clueless.

I snuck a peek at Maverick through my lashes. The taller boy was stoic as usual, not a smirk, smile, or frown graced his handsome, angular face. No more buzz cut for him. His coarse, brown hair had grown in thick and perfect, making him look even cuter than he already did.

It was everything I could do not to bare my teeth. Maverick was cute, but stupid me, I thought that just because he was introverted that meant he didn't *know* how cute he was. The guy played my attraction for him like a harp and one afternoon playing grabass with him almost got me kicked out of school.

I have something special for him. I have something special for all of them.

I cut eyes to Ezra as he sat straight-backed in his chair and dutifully pulled out his homework. He was still the most well-groomed boy I had ever seen in my life—nails perfect, hair slicked back, blazer buttoned up to the collar.

The boy who stole my first real kiss... and came for my mother in front of the whole school.

I wonder if they really thought they would get away with what they did to me.

The class door opened and I looked up as the AV club wheeled in the television. With a flick of the remote, Headmaster Evergreen was on the screen welcoming everyone to a new year.

We were thrown right in for all of our morning classes. No let's-get-to-know-each-other games. No going over the syllabus. I had moved up to Spanish II, English II, Advanced World History, and another semester of art, and those were just my Monday, Wednesday, and Friday classes.

Despite how fast my professors went, I felt good about this year. Last year had proven I could hold my own among geniuses, prodigies, and kids who went to private school their whole life.

I left World History with my head stuck in my textbook. *Can't believe the guy assigns a paper on the first day. I'm not sure I can spell Etruscan—*

"Val, where you running off to?" A shadow fell over my textbook and I pulled up quick. A kid I didn't know, but had seen around school last year, stood in front of me.

Dean? Darren? Who cares.

I gave him a filthy look. "Can I help you?"

"Yes, you can." He grinned wide enough to show off all his teeth. "The secret's out. You sell that ass for change and I'm happy to buy." He shrugged. "As long as you've taken care of that STD of course. So how about it? I was thinking five— No, four dollars for a fuck."

I raised a brow. "Are you offering to pay me for sex?"

He screwed up his face at the people watching like "Can you believe this girl?"

"Yes, I thought that was obvious."

"Alright. Just checking." Then I sidestepped him and kept walking.

"Hey! What time we hooking up?"

I didn't slow my stride. I rounded the corner and spotted my locker right away. Someone had been kind enough to cover it with joker cards, just in case I forgot for a solitary second that I was marked.

I ignored the cards as I tossed my new textbooks in my locker. They didn't faze me. My mind was on what was coming next: lunch.

There was a new lunchroom this year, but it would be filled with the same kids, and this time, they weren't driving me out.

I walked in and spared a glance around. This space looked exactly the same as the freshman cafeteria from the vaulted ceilings to the dais with a single table sitting upon it. The Knights had yet to make their appearance so I joined the lunch line, got my food tray, and found an empty table next to the window.

The taunts started up the moment I sat down, but I ignored it, focusing on my food. Sofia walked in a bit later with my old friends, Eric, Paisley, and Claire. Right behind them, were the Knights.

The boys sauntered inside single file with Ryder at the front, then Ezra, Jaxson, and Maverick taking the back. As usual, they skipped the line and went straight to their table. Four girls were right behind them with their lunch trays.

I shook my head. *Of course they expect to get away with everything. People cater to them like they have their whole lives. Nothing worse than giving a bunch of rich assholes more power.*

Dropping my eyes, I went back to my food as they pelted me with insults, not letting up until I finally tossed my tray and left.

MY BAGS WERE PACKED and ready to go the minute the bell rang ending classes. I shot up and bolted out the door while the rest of the class was still unzipping their backpacks. The reason why shouted for me when they stepped into the hall.

"Val, where are you running off to?" Isabella called. "We haven't had a chance to say hi yet."

I picked up the pace, and behind me I could hear the Diamonds doing the same. Those assholes were not going to make me late.

I took the stairs two at a time and raced out into the quad.

"Hey!"

They were seriously following me, and they were gaining—or one of them was. Axel pulled out ahead of the others and zeroed in on me, showing off just how he became Evergreen's track star.

I spun my head around and put on a burst of speed. *Almost ther—*

A hand grabbed my collar just as I yanked open the door. Axel and I tripped over the threshold and fell smack on the floor of the gym.

"Goodness, are you alright?"

I elbowed the idiot off me and scrambled to my feet. "I'm fine. I hope I'm not late. I can go right now."

A petite woman with a butterfly tat on her neck and hair in a multitude of braids blinked owlishly at me. "You're not late, but why don't you take a minute and catch your breath?"

The woman was bending to help Axel up when the rest of the Diamonds burst in.

"Valen— Oh." Natalie's shout was cut short by all of the eyes on her. A dozen people gathered on the floor of the gym, watching our little show.

The woman put Axel on his feet and then planted her hands on her hips. "Are you all here to try out?"

"Try out?" asked Airi. "Try out for what?"

"Then I'll take that as a no." The woman leveled a finger at the door. "These tryouts are closed. Leave now." She turned her back on them and gave me a smile at odds with her previous sharp tone. "But you can stay. Go get changed and then warm up. Dance team auditions start in five minutes."

"Dance?" Isabella's hiss brought a smile to my lips as I headed for the locker room. If she thought she was pissed now.

I changed quickly and then joined the group. The Diamonds were long gone so I was able to focus on warming up.

"Alright, everyone. For those who don't know, my name is Yvette, and should you make the team, I will be your coach. We do step, freestyle, hip-hop, and other forms of dance when we have guest instructors. We enter at least two competitions a semester as a group, more if I feel any of you can handle solo competitions."

I was bouncing on the heels of my feet. I was feeling everything she was saying and couldn't wait to show her what I could do. I would have been all over this team last year if I hadn't started school late, but going back and forth two hours to breastfeed Adam wasn't possible.

"So one by one you will show me your routines and then those who make the cut will find out tomorrow. Sound good?"

"Yes," I said along with the others.

"Let's get started then."

The first person stepped up and the rest of us moved to the bleachers. Most of the people here were juniors. The only people from my class were Tracy, Penelope, and... Eric.

I caught Eric looking at me from the corner of my eye, but his eyes slid away when I looked at him head-on. He took one end of the bleachers with the other sophomores while I took the other side. Thankfully, no one was any more interested in messing around than I was. We all focused on the tryouts and nailing our routines.

I took a break from mumbling steps to myself when Eric stood up.

Wow. He's good.

Good was putting it lightly. I had never seen Eric dance before but two minutes into his routine I knew he would be in. His moves were tight, inventive, and I caught a smile on Yvette's face. I knew there was more than a good chance that I would be on the team with people from my class, but I hadn't considered how I would handle being on the team with one of my old friends.

Eric sat down to applause and then I was next. I stood up and handed Yvette my music. She gave me a supportive smile as I backed up and got into position.

I had chosen an instrumental song of one of the Undisturbed's tracks. They had done a special collaboration with a reggae artist that resulted in a killer rhythm perfect for dancing. As soon as the music kicked off, I did.

I spun, dipped, shook, and even threw in a few flips I practiced in Sofia's guest room. I nailed every move, and when the song faded, I struck my final pose and fought to keep the grin off of my face.

"Very nice, Valentina," said Yvette. She lowered her clipboard to give me a smile. "You can get changed. I'll post the results tomorrow."

I nodded and set off for the changing rooms. I didn't stick around to watch the rest of tryouts. Stepping outside, I was relieved to see the Diamonds hadn't stuck around either. The quad was practically deserted, except for a few students laid out on the grass, soaking up the sun.

I pulled out my phone and texted Sofia on the way.

Me: Do you know the room numbers for the Knights and Diamonds?

She didn't text me back until I was in my room, shutting the door behind me.

Sofia: Why? What are you going to do?

Me: Not much without their passcodes. Just want to know where my enemies are.

Sofia: Okay. The boys are on the second floor. They have rooms next to each other. 202, 204, 206, 208. Natalie is 506. Isabella is 300. Airi is 112.

Right away I went to my desk and pulled out the list. I jotted their room numbers down next to their names.

Me: Thanks. You're the best.

Sofia: That is true.

I set aside my phone and picked up the list.

Time to get started.

I FINISHED MY HOMEWORK in record time—as in, I finished before dinner. Among the many things I didn't miss was how heavy our workload was.

I wanted a top-notch education with a side of privileged jackasses, I thought as I headed for the cafeteria. *And I got it.*

Dinner at Evergreen wasn't as intense as lunch. Students were allowed to pop in anytime from six to nine, and I usually avoided everyone by being there at six on the dot. I arrived at my usual time, but didn't go back to my room after picking up my tray.

My new spot next to the window was waiting for me, and I sat down and got comfortable. The zucchini pasta with stuffed bell peppers went down my throat fast. Sofia complained about how healthy we had to eat, but I couldn't get enough of this stuff.

I paused with my fork halfway to my mouth.

She's here.

Airi strode into the cafeteria with her head bent over her phone. She was alone.

I scarfed the rest of my food down while she got her tray and was up by the time she reached the door. Slowing down, I hung back as she walked down the hall and out into the quad. It wasn't until she reached the doors that I sped up.

I slipped inside and called for her. "Airi."

Airi stopped to peer over her shoulder. She scowled when she laid eyes on me. "What do you want?"

"I wanted to talk about last year." I tried for a smile and was lucky it didn't come across as a grimace. "Look, I know you guys didn't want to do the things you did to me."

The corner of her mouth rose with her grin. "Who says I didn't want to do it? You were so funny running off that stage bawling your eyes out."

With that, she gave me her back and kept walking. I jogged to catch up.

"We didn't have any problems before I was marked," I said as I fell in beside her. "Because we both had our own shit and couldn't be bothered."

Airi picked up the pace, passing my dorm to get to hers.

"I know you have better things to do than make my life miserable, so why don't we call a truce?"

Airi stopped in front of her door and moved her tray to one hand. She reached for the keypad. "How about no? Honestly, what are you even doing right now? This is a new level of pathetic."

Airi placed her finger on the first number then gave me a pointed look. I turned my head away and faint beeps sounded in my ear.

"I just thought I'd give you one last chance to end this," I continued, "because I'll be coming after the Diamonds and making sure you, Isabella, and your rabid bitch, Natalie, pay for what you did."

Airi choked. Her hand slipped on the doorknob and it swung shut in her face. "What did you just say?"

I gave her a salute. "Don't say I didn't warn you."

I took off before she could recover and was pushing into my room by the time the insults started. Hurrying to my bed, I unbuttoned my shirt and took out the camera.

Come on, come on, come on. Please tell me I got it.

I was wrong about it being hard to smile. This one came with no problem. I watched the screen as Airi typed in her passcode and the grin came to my lips.

I did warn her.

Chapter Three

I was first to Wheeldon's class the next morning. If I was going to be surrounded by so many enemies, then it wouldn't be good for me to follow them into a room after they've had a chance to plot.

Isabella, Natalie, and Airi shot me poisonous looks when they came through the door. The Knights weren't nearly so predictable.

I stiffened when Jaxson, Ryder, and Maverick filed in. They all knew I was coming after them now; I wondered how that would change things.

They were already making your life miserable. What more can they do?

Maverick turned down my row and went to his seat without sparing me a glance. Ryder didn't pretend he couldn't see me. The bastard winked at me before taking his seat next to Airi. I looked away when they leaned in and started whispering about something—that rare smile hanging on his lips.

I shifted away—

—and jumped when Jaxson leaned over me.

"Ooh, why so nervous?" Jaxson rested his elbows on my desk and leaned in close enough that I was engulfed in his spicy sweet scent. Jaxson had a problem sticking to the uniform rules and today was no different. His shirt was only half buttoned, giving me a straight view to his hard chest. "If my sweet Valentina is going to take us down, she'll have to be tougher than that."

I tore my eyes up and met his. "I was never sweet, and there is no 'if.' I will take you down."

"If you say so." His tone told me everything I needed to know about how seriously he was taking this. Jaxson reached up and pushed the hair behind my ear like he had so many times before. His fingers lingered on the shell of my ear, following the curve down to my neck.

"I heard you got off with Connor Masterson behind the sports complex." I tensed, and not just because of what he was saying. His finger was tracing a lazy pattern on my neck and it was everything I could do not to shiver under his touch. "He said you gave him a good deal too. You know I've been trying to get with you for months. It's starting to hurt my feelings that you're going with everyone else but me."

"When are you going to give that a rest?" I hissed through gritted teeth. "I don't sell my body."

He shrugged. "You also said you were a virgin and we all know that was a lie."

Smack!

The slap rang out through the classroom, causing a dozen eyes to swivel to us.

Jaxson straightened slowly. The red handprint stark on his cheek as the grin melted off his face.

Molten anger rolled through my veins. The hand that slapped him shook. Forget long, drawn-out revenge plots; I was ready to leap over the desk and claw his eyes out.

"I'll admit I deserve that," Jaxson began, "but you only get one for free."

"Excuse me." The classroom door slammed shut with a bang. Wheeldon's bulk was even more intimidating coupled with the glare he was giving me and Jaxson. "Do we have a problem here?"

"Nope," Jaxson said easily. "All good here."

He loped off but the eyes on me remained. I yanked out my textbook and buried my nose in reading rather than look at anyone.

I shouldn't have hit him. That wasn't how I wanted to do this, but I couldn't stand him throwing in my face that I wasn't a virgin. That had been taken from me.

I didn't lift my head until the door opened again for the AV students to wheel in the television.

"Good morning, sophomores." Ezra's charming voice filled the room. "Just a few announcements to kick off our year. This weekend marks the first football game against the Lancaster Prep Falcons. I'm sure everyone will be there to cheer Maverick and the Kings to victory."

Maverick inclined his head to accept the applause that rang out. The guy was quiet and mellow in the classroom, but a beast on the field. The Kings were undefeated under him.

"Next week we vote on the theme of this year's homecoming dance. Your options are: Under the Sea, Alice in Wonderland, An Evening in Paris, or Artic Paradise. The dance will be held at the end of the month, and like before, students will be given one afternoon off to..."

I tuned out the rest. What did I care about silly little dances?

I was first out of the door when the bell rang. My next class was art with Scarlett and I was actually looking forward to it.

She beamed when I walked through the door. "Valentina. It's so good to see you." She stood and came around the desk to enfold me in a hug. She looked the same as she always did—freckles dusting her cheeks and paint splattered on her overalls. She pulled back and rubbed my forearms. "How have you been?"

"Good."

She lifted a brow. "Really? I know you had a tough time of it last year. Honestly, I was surprised you came back."

I shrugged. "I wasn't going to let a few bullies control my life."

Scarlett squeezed my arm. "You're a strong girl." Scarlett had been one of the few people to show me any kindness last year.

"Speaking of coming back," she went on. "Why did you choose art as your elective? I didn't think you were passionate about it."

"It was either this or public speaking, and I'm never standing on stage in front of my class again."

She winced. "Oh. Right. Well, grab a workstation and we'll get started."

Unlike last year, the room wasn't taken up by stools and easels. This time individual work tables lined the space in neat rows. I went to one at the front and set my bag next to the stool.

"Alright, class, welcome to Art Studio II," Scarlett began. "This year will be different. We're shifting away from painting and instead working with other forms of expression like sculpting, ceramics, and drawing. So take out your textbooks and read chapter one, please. Afterward, we'll discuss."

I chanced a look around as I pulled out my book.

No Maverick.

He hadn't signed up to take art this semester, and neither had the other Knights. Clearly, it had been a good idea to choose Scarlett's class. This would be a rare break from all the craziness.

After my final class let out, I headed back to homeroom to get my phone. I hated Evergreen's policy of keeping them locked up all day, but I had as much a chance of getting the headmaster to change his mind as I did of getting rid of the mark.

Wheeldon didn't look up from his desk when I came in. I crossed over to the lockbox where he kept my cell captive and fished it out. It buzzed in my hand the moment I palmed it.

Glancing at the screen, I froze.

Another look at Wheeldon confirmed he couldn't give a flying fart what I was doing so I didn't waste a second pulling the message up.

000-5673: I can't do everything you want, but most of it won't be a problem.

My fingers flew across the screen.

Me: What can't you do?

000-5673: Hacking into Evergreen's network is impossible. It was designed by Marcus Beaumont himself. People better than me have tried and it doesn't get much better than me.

I deflated. *Damn it. What now?*

Me: What about Maverick Beaumont's laptop? Also impossible?

000-5673: Maybe not. Doubt there's military-grade encryptions on a teenage boy's sticky laptop. But if he's half as good as his father, it'll still be tough. That will cost extra.

I chewed my lip, thinking. I knew Maverick was good. He reduced my old laptop to a pile of scrap metal in minutes, but if there was even a chance this guy... or girl... could do it then I would pay whatever it took.

Me: Money is not an issue.

000-5673: My favorite sentence.

Me: What about the phones? The videos?

000-5673: Won't be a problem.

Me: And none of this will be traced back to me?

000-5673: Like I said, it doesn't get much better than me.

Me: Fine. What do I call you?

000-5673: Make up whatever name you like. I'll send you the account information now. I receive payment within the hour or the deal is off.

Me: Also fine. How much do I owe you?

My eyebrows shot up my forehead at the next text message. I had asked to be put in touch with the best hacker they could find, so it shouldn't have surprised me that the best wasn't cheap, but still—

It's worth it.

I blew out a breath, steeling my resolve. It was worth it. Taking down this school and everyone in it was never going to be easy, but I'd empty every cent in my bank account if it meant making them feel a fraction of what I felt on that stage.

I slipped my phone in my bag, turned to go, and found Isabella blocking the door.

My eyes flicked to Wheeldon who was still absorbed with whatever was on his computer.

"Move, Isabella."

She didn't even twitch. "What are you trying to pull, Moon?"

I walked up to her and stopped when we were inches apart. "I'm trying to go back to my dorm. How about you?"

Her eyes narrowed into slits. "Don't think I don't see what you're doing trying out for the dance team. You getting on doesn't mean anything."

"I got on the team?" A smile lit my face as a scowl crossed hers. "Nice."

"You can't challenge my title," she hissed. "You're marked. The Diamonds will sooner cut off your hair than put a crown on it."

Shaking my head, I replied, "Not everything is about you and your vicious clique. Did you ever think that it's not that I want your title, it's just I want you to spend the rest of our time here knowing that you don't deserve it." Isabella's face tightened with every word. "That the girl from the Wakefield slum who learned to dance in front of a television is better than you."

"You don't know ballet!"

I waved my finger. "It's not the best ballet dancer," I said, repeating something Sofia told me long ago. "It's the best dancer period. And if you're so good—classically trained by top instructors since you were in the womb—then a little step and hip-hop will be nothing to you."

"It is nothing." She bent down and got in my face. "Just like you are. I'm not worried about you."

"Really?" I pressed my finger to her temple. "Then why is that vein twitching so hard?"

Isabella seized my hand before I could pull back. "Don't—!"

"Ladies."

Our heads whipped around to face Wheeldon. The man spoke without looking away from the screen. "Leave my classroom now."

I didn't need to be told twice. I yanked my wrist out of her grasp and moved around her to the door.

Isabella didn't follow me out so I was able to make it back to my dorm with no more drama. I got busy putting the rest of my plan into motion the moment I was inside.

Not being able to hack into Evergreen's system was a setback, but one I had a plan B for. If Alex, as I was now going to call them, couldn't get in and erase my presence from the security cameras or get me room passcodes, I would just have to get creative.

"I HATE THAT WE'RE NOT in the same class."

Sofia reached over and plucked my angel food cupcake off my plate. She had half of it in her mouth before I got out—

"Hey!"

She chewed unrepentantly. "I deserve it. I'm sad."

"But we're sad about the same thing, cupcake thief." I got back at her by spearing a piece of her roasted salmon.

"You can have that—way too healthy for me." She placed her tray on the tiny reclaimed wooden table and pulled her legs up onto the couch. We were sitting in our spot on the roof. Despite everything, I couldn't deny how beautiful it was out here with no lights or traffic to take away from the calm of night. Sofia sighed. "It'll be harder to let you know if I hear anything about you."

"Have you heard anything?"

She shook her head. "Nothing except you getting on the dance team and trying to challenge Isabella. Is that true?"

"I always wanted to get on the team, but I won't lie, pissing off Ballerina Bella is a big bonus."

"People overheard you to Ryder. It's getting around that you're planning to get back at the Knights."

I shrugged. "If people didn't know already, they would soon enough."

"Are you sure there is nothing I can do to help you?"

"Sof, I love you. That's why I'm keeping you out of this. The best thing you can do is warn me if someone else plots to sabotage my homework or throw me down the stairs."

"Don't joke about that."

I crumpled my napkin and tossed it back on my tray. "I have to go. There's a couple things I need to do before bed." We hugged and then I grabbed my things and left.

The quad was eerily quiet that night. There wasn't a soul about, making my sneaking feel shadier. I peeked at the security cameras on my way into my room.

They make things difficult, but tonight you may help me too.

Lying on my bed was my change of clothes. I quickly got into them and then turned to face the mirror as I put on the final touch.

Wow. I really look like a guy.

Staring back at me was a figure in a yellow blazer, plaid pants, and a dark brown, bowl-cut wig. The wig had been easy enough to get my hands on. You can have stuff like that delivered. The hard part had been hunting down an Evergreen boys' uniform online and getting someone to sell it to me. I thought at first about sneaking one out of the laundry, but I figured the boy would notice an entire uniform going missing.

No, this was perfect. This was all I needed for Airi Tanaka.

Well, almost everything...

I stepped away from the mirror and reached under my bed. The suitcase holding everything I needed for this year sat innocently beneath my sheets. It took me seconds to dig inside and find what I was looking for.

Time to go.

Silently, I eased open my bedroom window and slipped outside. If any good could have come out of falling down the stairs, it was that being put on the first floor had saved me a lot of headache.

My feet were soundless on the freshly mowed grass as I skirted around the building to the front door. Taking a deep breath, I strolled inside and passed through the lobby to the first-floor dorms. I kept my head slightly lowered, highly aware of the cameras that tracked me.

I passed my room and stepped boldly up to Airi's door. I didn't hesitate as I tapped in the passcode and heeded the soft chime to step inside.

Closing the door behind me, I leaned against it, letting my eyes adjust to the darkness. Airi's room cleared before me and I resisted the urge to whistle. I thought my room was nice, but it was nothing compared to what this rich, pampered princess had done to hers.

An expensive throw rug took up most of the space. It matched perfectly with the plush, imperial sheets the lovely Airi was sleeping soundly on.

I approached her bed, eyes locked on her. Airi's face was half covered by the beauty mask, but the same couldn't be said for the beautiful hair that covered the pillow. I once complimented her luscious, jet-black waterfall. It was obvious to everyone that Airi took special care of her hair and never left her dorm unless it was perfect.

I wanted to cut every strand of that perfect hair from her evil little head. Watch her weep and shake when she found herself as bald as her little boyfriend Ryder was. I wanted to... but scissors weren't what I brought.

I held out my hand, and the metal head of the hammer glinted in the scant moonlight seeping in through the window.

I gazed down at Airi. She looked so peaceful, almost sweet, as she made soft wheezing noises in her sleep. I reached out with the hammer, and closed my fingers around the neck of the violin.

It's sweet that she keeps it right by her bed on the nightstand.

Backing away, I moved over to the window and unlatched it. I prayed to every deity I had ever heard of that the hinges wouldn't squeak as I gently inched it open.

Only when it was big enough for me to slip through did I heave myself outside and take off.

Adrenaline hammered in my chest as I raced to the outside of my bedroom and pulled out the box I had placed next to the window.

Hurry, hurry, hurry!

The warning skittered up my spine and latched on to my ear, shouting at me as I picked up speed and fled to the back of the sports center. I needed privacy to do this, somewhere that no one would overhear. The woods were out, so that left our—and Coach Panzer's—secret spot.

I burst onto the roof and let the door slam shut behind me. My lungs were working overtime, but it wasn't fear or anger or pain. I was smiling. I was smiling so wide my cheeks hurt from the strange feeling. Placing my hand on my chest, I marveled at the lack of tightness. Was this the key to pushing back against the darkness?

I let the violin slip through my fingers and crash to the floor. The first splinter appeared in the wood and was swiftly followed by dozens more when I brought the hammer down.

I let loose. Smashing, beating, and pulverizing the stupid thing into a million pieces of wood. When I was satisfied, I carefully picked up the bits of violin and placed them into the box. A thought occurred to me as I closed the top.

Maybe it's not about pushing back the darkness... but about letting it in.

I WOKE EARLY THE NEXT morning, showered, dressed, and tried harder to accessorize with the banana uniform. I came away with my peridot pendant and matching earrings. My hair I swept back and wrangled into a small bun. Only when I was perfect did I gather my things and leave the dorms.

There was barely anyone about the quad that morning. Except for a couple of people sitting on the benches with their homework, there was no one to notice me. I had never been so glad that Evergreen only had security cameras in the dorms—something I had privately felt was so the Spades could move about unnoticed, breaking into people's lockers, but now it would come in handy for my sneaking too.

I traveled upstairs to Wheeldon's empty classroom, placed the box on Airi's desk, and left the way I came without a break in my step. I walked to breakfast with the smile back on my face.

"—TELLING YOU IT'S JUST gone."

I glanced up from my work as the Diamonds filed into homeroom. Isabella led the way with Airi on her tail, and today, she was less than perfect. There was a black streak on the front of her yellow dress, and her hair had been pulled into a messy ponytail, but the most telling feature was the red around her eyes.

"I looked everywhere for it," she cried. "I tore my room apart, but it's nowhere. How could that happen?"

"Maybe you left it in the music room," Natalie offered. Natalie's look was the complete opposite of Airi's. Her uniform dress hung perfectly on her full frame, and the multitude of earrings adorning her ears shone in the artificial lights.

"But I didn't— What's this?"

Airi paused when she finally noticed the present on her desk—purple wrapping paper with a neat black bow waiting for her to look inside.

I didn't still my hand. My pencil continued across my paper even though I was writing gibberish now. I didn't care about the mess. I watched Airi through my lashes as she lifted the top of the present and—

"Ahhhhhh!"

Airi's scream jerked Wheeldon out of his seat. "For the love of— What's wrong?!"

Airi didn't speak for the sobs wracking her body. I lost sight of her as half the class sprang out of their seat to see what happened.

I didn't move. Instead, I went back to my homework for real and pretended I couldn't see Maverick watching me out of the corner of my eye.

I knew how much that violin meant to Airi. I had overheard her brag that the precious gift she had gotten from her grandfather was what started her love of the instrument. She told everyone that it was the lucky charm that allowed her to nail every performance. That she had risen to the top because of that violin.

Cutting that gorgeous mane would have been satisfying, but hair grows back. It wouldn't have made nearly the same impact as taking away that irreplaceable item. It seemed harsh, and there was a moment where I thought I shouldn't do it, but then I remembered the website.

I remembered Airi smirking about putting me online and listing all the sex acts I would do for pennies. I remembered the men who emailed me because of her and told me in horrific, graphic detail the things they wanted to do to an underage girl.

I remembered the nightmares that followed and the nights I woke up screaming as vivid memories of my rape seeped back into my mind. Compared to that, breaking that stupid fucking violin was letting her off easy.

Airi cried all through homeroom until Wheeldon finally took pity on her and told Isabella to escort her to the nurse. I left when the bell rang, ignoring Maverick's eyes on me.

I felt stronger as I wandered the halls. The taunts about my weight and offers to sleep with me didn't stop, but I didn't feel powerless anymore. I couldn't change what made this place so rotten, but I could fight back. The Spades—whoever they were—would see they couldn't break me.

I left my last class of the day and made one pit stop to drop my second cam in my gym locker. After, I headed out for my bookbag and textbooks, my mind on what we had for lunch. The best thing about Evergreen was that the chef never made the same thing twice.

I leaned half in my locker, licking my lips as I scrolled through the recipe for avocado chili steak tacos with honey cinnamon sweet potatoes.

Oh my gosh. Yum. I have to make this for Mom when I go home.

"If you think that is good..."

The smile froze on my face.

"...just wait until you taste me."

I felt his heat against my body before I saw him. Jaxson placed his hand on my back, and trailed a path as he got between me and my locker. He grinned at me. "I forgive you for yesterday, baby. Made no sense to insult you while we were handling business."

I heard snickering and glanced around me. Maverick, Ezra, and Ryder stood a few feet from us—watching with differing looks on their faces while the rest of the students scattered about the hall looked on.

"But I can't keep chasing after you when so many more are free and willing." His finger slipped under the band of my skirt and he tugged me closer. "This is your last chance so how about it? I'll pay whatever you want."

I looked into those sparkling blue eyes, breathing heavy. In spite of what he said, this wouldn't be the last time. They all loved harassing me and making disgusting remarks about how I was able to afford the things I did. This was never going to stop.

"Okay." The word was out of my mouth before I could think harder about it. "Let's do it."

Jaxson blinked. "What? Do what?"

I rolled my eyes. "Fuck, obviously. Isn't that what we're talking about?" I broke from his grasp and brushed him aside to put the rest of the things in my locker. I glanced at the other Knights while I slammed it shut. Their expressions matched now. They all watched me with disbelief as I reached for Jaxson.

"Valen—"

"Shut up and let's get this over with." I snagged his collar and dragged him after me. Jaxson tripped behind me as I led him down the hallway and straight for the custodian's closet. "This should do the trick."

I unceremoniously tossed him inside. I closed the door behind us with a snap. Turning, I ended up inches from Jaxson's chest. His shirt was unbuttoned as always and the smell of him was filling my mind and the small space we were in. There was nowhere for me to go, barely space for us to move. I took a deep breath and reached for the buttons still doing their job.

"Valentina, what are you doing?" This wasn't Jaxson's usual devil-may-care voice. He grabbed one of my wrists, but I shook him off.

"It'll be a thousand bucks," I said matter-of-factly. I got the last button free and swept the shirt off his shoulders in one smooth move.

Bare-chested, he gaped at me while I tried to keep my eyes on his face. There were a lot of things I hated about Jaxson Van Zandt, but how fit he was wasn't one of them.

"A thousand?" he cried. "Are you insane?"

I cocked my hip and placed my hand on it. "The rates go up for assholes and you said you'd pay whatever I asked." I smiled. "Or were you just talking big in front of your friends? I knew you were a fake. I meet your bluff and now you're shrinking like a virgin." I reached for the doorknob. "You've had your chance so I better not hear about this again."

Jaxson's hand flashed out before I could take a step. "Fine," he growled. "A thousand."

The next thing I felt was Jaxson's hand on my shoulder. He turned me around and cupped the back of my head as he tilted my neck back. My pulse picked up speed knowing what was coming next. Jaxson brought his lips down on mine—

—and once again caught my cheek when I twisted away.

"Kissing is off the table," I announced. "I'd charge you extra for that too, but the truth is I just flat out don't want you slobbering on me."

Jaxson's eyes snapped open. "You don't what?"

I ignored him and dropped to my knees. My hands were rough as I tugged on his belt. I tried not to think about what I was doing as I threw the belt over my head, then unbuttoned his pants. Jaxson didn't stop me as I pulled the pants down around his ankles, and then with shaky fingers, his boxers.

I swallowed hard.

Jaxson's member hung centimeters from my face. It wasn't what I expected in so many ways, and before my eyes it stiffened until the distance between us grew shorter.

Taking a breath, I leaned in and carefully dug through his pockets until my fingers closed over his phone. I set it on the floor and soundlessly pushed it under a mop bucket.

"Wow, I get it now," I said when it was safely hidden. "If this was what I was working with, I'd be an insecure ass too." I got to my feet and smirked into his astonished face. "I'll have to fake it for this one because there's no way that little fellow is going to get me off. Make it another thousand."

Jaxson's face twisted. "Shut up!" He grabbed my waist and spun me around. In a breath, his hand was under my skirt and hooking through my panties. He pulled them down and I sucked in a breath when the cool air hit my bare backside. I sucked it in, but couldn't let it out. I felt the tightening in my chest, squeezing and squeezing.

Jaxson, on the other hand, was breathing hard. I could sense his frustration even though the hand he placed on my thigh was gentle. The breathing got louder until it was made real against my ear. Jaxson pressed his body against me, and before I could think he captured my ear between his teeth.

"Eek." The small squeak sprung unbidden from my lips and I clapped my hand over my mouth to prevent another one. My nerve endings were exploding with electricity.

Jaxson's hands traveled up my skin enticing my knees to quiver, and not because I didn't want this. The pressure built in the only place his hand could be going and I thought fast.

"Are you in yet?" I demanded. "How am I supposed to tell?"

Jaxson's hand flew off my thigh inches from his destination. "You know what! Fuck this!"

I listened as he hastily pulled up his pants and shoved his way out of the broom closet. I pulled up my panties the moment the door slammed shut and tried to remember how to breathe.

I was wrong, I thought as I gasped. *Letting the darkness in doesn't fix everything. It doesn't fix me.*

Chapter Four

I set Jaxson's phone on my bedside table and pulled my legs up onto the bed. I had showered, but all the scrubbing and hot water in the world couldn't rid my body of the feeling of Jaxson's fingers ghosting over my thigh. I couldn't stop thinking about what almost happened. I couldn't stop thinking about the fact that for a moment I was going to *let* it happen.

I knew I was going to have to get creative to get Jaxson's phone. If I had just slipped it out of the phone box, he would have known it was stolen, and he would have probably looked at me. I wanted him to think it had just gone missing, but I shouldn't have gone so far to make it happen.

From now on there has to be rules, and this has to be one of them. I don't use my sexuality to get revenge.

That was a rule I didn't have trouble accepting. It was easy to go too far, I had been hurt so badly, but with a history like mine; I needed to have limits.

That settled, I reached for my phone and texted Alex.

Me: I've got the phone. How do I get in?

Phones these days were locked up tighter than government secrets and Jaxson's was no different. I only had to wait about ten minutes for Alex to get me back.

Alex: I'll send you instructions. If this guy has on his phone what you think he does, then this will be big.

Me: I know he does. And it will.

Alex sent me the step-by-step list to break into a smartphone, but even so, it took me half the night. Eventually, I had to stop and do my homework before that kept me up the rest of the night too. Once I knocked out my World History assignment, I went back to the phone. An hour later, I was in.

I didn't waste a moment in going to his recordings. My face almost cracked in half with my smile as I scrolled through hours and hours of secretly recorded sets. I recalled Jaxson saying once that he liked to sneak a snippet of the bands and artists that came to his father's studio. I'd feel bad about what I was going to do, but Jaxson had known what he was doing was wrong and had done it anyway.

Just like he planned every moment of humiliating me and revealing I had an STD for the whole world to see. It had only been pure chance that Mom never saw the trending video before the headmaster had them all taken down, but the same couldn't be said for a few of the kids I used to go to school with. They hunted me down on Facebook and filled my messages with "Diseased Slut" until I finally blocked them all.

I didn't feel sympathy for Jaxson Van Zandt. I only hoped I was there to see Jaxson's face when it all came out.

I WAS UP EARLY AGAIN the next morning and slipping into my homeroom with no one the wiser. Jaxson's cell was put back into the phone box safe and sound.

I left and hung out in the library until the clock told me I had minutes to the start of homeroom. Walking through the halls, I spotted the Knights ahead of me deep in conversation. I didn't pick up the pace until they stepped through the door.

"Shit." Jaxson reached into the box just as I stepped inside. He pulled out his phone. "You were right, Ricky. I forgot it in class." Jaxson frowned as he looked at the screen. "Damn. Papa Van Zandt was blowing me up. I've got like fifteen missed calls from him."

"What's up?" asked Ezra.

I wandered down my row, keeping one eye on the group.

"No clue." Jaxson tapped the screen and pressed the phone to his ear.

"Excuse me, Mr. Van Zandt." Wheeldon rose from his seat. "Phone away now."

Jaxson turned his frown on him. "Chill, dude. It's my dad. Something's up."

"I don't care what's up. I said put the phone away."

He spun on him. "You know, I'm getting real sick of you!"

Everyone—including me—froze at his shout. My eyes snapped to Wheeldon, wondering what Evergreen's newest teacher was going to do.

The man's muscles bulged as he balled his hands into fists. "You're going to get real sick of detention if you ever speak to me like that again."

"You—!"

Ezra clapped his hand over his friend's mouth. "Sorry, sir," he said as he hooked an arm around Jaxson and tugged him away. "He's just worried about his father. It won't happen again."

Leave it to the Knights' resident poster boy to save the day, I thought as Ezra hauled Jaxson to his seat. Halfway, Jaxson looked across the rows and our eyes connected. Bright spots of color stained his cheeks before he tore his eyes away. It was only milliseconds before I did the same. I pressed my hand to my face, feeling the heat spread through my palm. I don't think I will ever get the sight of Jaxson naked out of my head.

He got Jaxson in his seat and everyone settled in except Ezra who took off to do the announcements.

I held my breath all through my morning classes as I waited for the shit to hit the fan. I was partly cursing the no-phone policy, but I'd just have to make sure I was in homeroom when he finally picked it up.

Walking out of English II, I turned my thought to food as I headed for my locker.

"Miss Moon."

I pulled up short and peered over my shoulder. I stopped dead at seeing Headmaster Evergreen standing beside a red-rimmed Airi.

Goodness. The guy left his office. This must be serious.

To confirm it, Evergreen crooked his finger. "Miss Moon, my office, now."

I cut eyes to Airi and the look I received back was nothing short of venomous. I didn't bother to ask questions and followed them back to Evergreen's office. We walked inside and I paused again. There was a man I had never seen before standing behind the headmaster's desk.

"Thank you for coming, Gus," said Evergreen. "Ladies, you can have a seat."

So this is the infamous Gus.

I had heard this man's name many times but had never met him. The person who headed up the security team that watched us through the cameras and employed people like Noemi. In person, he was just an average-looking tall guy in a staff uniform.

"What is this about?" I asked when Evergreen sat down.

"You know what this is about," Airi spat from my other side. She leveled a trembling finger at me. "It was her, Headmaster. She destroyed my violin."

I gaped at her. "I did what? What are you talking about?"

Airi's eyes were wild. "Don't mess with me, you stupid bitch!"

"That is enough of that, Miss Tanaka," Evergreen cut in.

"But, sir, I know it was her." Airi shifted toward him. "She threatened me the day before and then my violin is stolen and smashed. That's supposed to be a coincidence?"

Evergreen looked at me. "What do you say to these accusations? Did you threaten Miss Tanaka?"

"I didn't threaten anyone, and I definitely didn't steal any violin." I made a face. "How would I have done that anyway?"

"You got into my room somehow," Airi shot back.

I scoffed. "Are you crazy? I didn't go into your room."

Gus came alive. "We can settle this right now. I have the security videos." He handed the headmaster a disk and we fell silent as he put it in the computer. He didn't bother to turn the monitor so Airi and I could see, so I watched Evergreen's face. The seconds ticked down as I waited for Evergreen to speak, react, something.

Suddenly, his brows shot up to his hairline. Airi noticed the same because she leaned forward in her seat. "You saw her," she stated. "I told you she did it. I want her expelled, and my family will be pressing charges."

Evergreen didn't say anything for a minute. "Miss Tanaka," he began, "are you aware of Evergreen's policy regarding those of opposite genders going into each other's rooms?"

"What? What does that have to—"

"Can you explain to me why there is a boy going into your bedroom on the night in question?" Evergreen's voice was so chilly I swore I could see his breath. He twisted the monitor around and there on the screen was a short-haired figure in a boy's uniform.

Airi's jaw worked but no sounds came out.

"Miss Tanaka, this is a serious offense." Evergreen removed his hands from the screen to steeple them beneath his face. This was a pose I knew well. "I'm afraid I can't ignore this. The punishment for having a boy in your room is—"

Airi quickly found her voice. "Punishment?" she cried. "Why would I be punished?! I don't have a clue who that guy is."

Gus stepped forward. "He clearly uses your passcode to get in. If you don't know him, how was he able to enter your room?"

"I don't know," she replied, waving her hands. "But I have no idea who that is." She cut furious eyes to me. "And what about her? She must know that guy. She must have gotten him to break into my room."

"Impossible," Gus spoke up, "unless she or he had your passcode to begin with. Did you share your code with Miss Moon?"

"Of course, I didn't," she snapped. "Why are you asking me all of these questions when you should be speaking to her?!"

Evergreen stayed fixed on Airi. "We can see who enters your room and it is not Miss Moon. If someone truly has managed to steal your passcode and did so to destroy your possessions, then that person will be found and subjected to the harshest possible punishment."

Evergreen finally acknowledged me. "You may go, Miss Moon."

I stood up before he finished the sentence.

"You can't let her go!" Airi sounded near tears again. "I know she had something to do with this!"

"If that is true, the investigation will bear that out." Evergreen pointed at the door. "Leave, Miss Moon."

I left. The door closed with a soft click that I was somehow able to hear even among Airi's renewed shouting.

"I need to speak to my son now."

I looked up and almost fell back against the door. *Hera help me, that's Levi Van Zandt!*

I want to say I wasn't staring like an open-mouthed fool but that was exactly what I was doing. Levi was even cooler in person—in spite of looking spitting mad. The leather-clad, boot-wearing middle-aged man was tapping those boots so hard I could almost dance a beat to them.

"Of course, Mr. Van Zandt," said the receptionist. "But he's at lunch right now if you'd like to wait."

Levi's response was to sweep out of the room.

"Mr. Van Zandt? Mr. Van Zandt!" The receptionist stuck to yelling from her desk, but I didn't. I darted through the doors and trailed Jaxson's dad as he stalked toward the lunchroom. Levi didn't seem to notice me behind him which was just as well. I didn't want to slow him down.

I picked up speed when he reached the double doors and was only a few feet behind him when he burst into the cafeteria. Our eyes both zeroed in on the same spot.

Jaxson sat at his table on the dais, laughing at something the girl on his lap was saying. I recognized her as one of the girls who brought the Knights lunch every day. Levi was halfway to the table when Jaxson finally noticed him.

He dropped his smile quick. "Dad? Dad, what's wrong?" He got to his feet despite his lap being occupied and sent the girl to the floor.

Levi's boots clomped on the steps to the dais, ringing in the rapidly quieting cafeteria.

"Da— Ow!"

Levi seized his son's ear and dragged him off the platform.

"Dad! Stop!" Jaxson stumbled along after his father, face screwed up and practically neon red. "Dad!"

"Do you have any idea what you've done?!" Levi roared. He gave his son's head a shake. "What were you thinking?!"

"What did I do?!"

Jaxson was still repeating that question after they disappeared through the doors. My mouth was still hanging open.

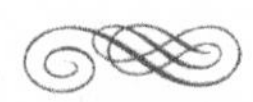

SOFIA SHOOK HER HEAD in disbelief. "I can't believe this. The unreleased albums of *five* bands and artists have hit YouTube. The feed is blowing up."

I reclined into the couch cushions and leaned my head back to the sky. "Jaxson's dad was blowing up. I think the entire campus heard him chewing the guy out."

"Of course, what Jaxson did was every kind of stupid, and then to go posting it online." I turned in time to see her shake her head. "I heard from Paisley that he's saying he was hacked, but he can't pretend he didn't record the songs in the first place."

That night we were back in our spot with our dinners on our laps. There was only one thing on our minds to discuss.

"I've heard him brag about it," I said.

Sofia sighed. "Jaxson really did it this time. Who knows what is going to happen to Interstellar Records because of this."

"What?" My head shot off the couch. "What do you mean?"

"Val, it's all over the feed." She handed me her phone so I could see for myself. "These artists sign contracts. They've got deals and money hanging on these albums. They might sue the label."

My mouth fell open for the second time that day. I scrolled through her feed as dread filled my bones. It was true. Her page was on fire with news titles like "Is This The End of Interstellar?"

"But I didn't want this," I blurted. "I never wanted to hurt his dad or the label."

Sofia's eyes bugged out. "What did you just say? Val, did you have something to do with this?"

I gave her a look that seemed to say it all.

"Val! How?"

"I got into Jaxson's phone and leaked the audio files, but only he was supposed to get in trouble," I added quickly at the shock on her face. "He deserves everything that's coming to him for this, and I hope he felt a fraction of the humiliation I did when his dad dragged him out in front of everyone."

"But, Val." She gently took the phone from me. "This has gotten bigger than him now."

"I know, and I'm sorry. Really, I am, but I can't take it back. Hopefully they'll realize that it's not the label's fault."

"I hope so too."

The two of us fell into a silence that I didn't know how to break—that was until I noticed the corners of Sofia's mouth twitching.

"What are you smiling about?"

She stifled a giggle. "That was really funny though. Levi pulled him out by his ear like he was a poopy-pants toddler who drew on the walls."

Before I knew it, we were both howling. Every time I tried to catch my breath she would say "poopy-pants" and I was at it again. I fell on Sofia's lap, trying to hold on to this mood for a little longer.

She patted my head. "You going to tell me about the rest of this plan yet?"

I was expecting this question and was ready for it. "I can tell you part of it right now, because it involves you."

"What do you need me to do?"

"The masquerade dance from last year. Can you get as many photos as possible from that night so I—"

"—can find the person in the red-and-white mask who fought with Ryder," she finished. "Good idea, but if they have their mask on in the pictures, how will you know who it is?"

"I can still narrow it down. Hair color, skin color, height, if they wore a tux or dress. I just need something to go on." I sat up and shifted to look her in the eyes. "Every single second since I found that card in my locker, I've been going over that night.

"The Spades marked me right after it happened, but neither Ryder or that mystery person came forward to reveal what happened. They knew what I saw, but that only happens if Ryder or the mystery person told them, or they *are* them. Either way, one of them is connected to the Spades, but if I'm honest, I don't think it's Ryder."

"Why not? He's proven that he hates you."

"Exactly. The guy can't stand me which makes me wonder why, if he had the power to mark me, he didn't do it the second he saw me. He wouldn't have needed to wait until I stumbled on him in the woods."

Sofia paused, chewing her lip as she thought. "That is a good point."

"I need to find out who the other person is and that is the most important thing you can do to help me."

She nodded. "Okay, I'll do it. You know I have your back."

"Thank you." I fell back into her lap and got comfortable. "Now... I need to tell you exactly what I did to get Jaxson's phone..."

I ALMOST SLEPT THROUGH my alarm the next morning. Between the early mornings, and Sofia refusing to let me go to bed until I went over every second with Jaxson in the broom closet at least a dozen times, I didn't get to sleep until almost three in the morning.

I dragged myself into homeroom cursing this blasted school for not allowing us to drink coffee. We weren't even allowed black tea.

I noticed the eyes on me as I put my phone away, but I refused to make eye contact with their dirty looks.

What do they have to be so mad about? It's not like they're innocent. Not like I was.

Chancing a look, I glanced at Jaxson while I took my seat and almost felt a twinge of sympathy for him. Almost.

Gone was the cocky smile, half-buttoned shirt, and twinkling blue eyes. His homework sat before him while he stared unseeingly at the back of Ryder's head. The guy looked so out of it; he probably wouldn't twitch if the fire alarm went off.

I lowered my head and pulled out my own homework. I was done with Jaxson. His name was crossed off my list, and as long as he didn't do anything else, it would stay that way.

I got through the rest of my classes thinking only of what would happen when they let out. The moment the final bell rang I was out of my seat racing toward the sports complex. Yvette waved at me from the bleachers when I stepped inside.

"Hello, Valentina," she said as she stepped down. "You're the first to arrive so why don't you get changed and start warming up."

"Okay."

I headed to the locker room to do as she asked and ten minutes later was stretching out on the mat. My forehead touched my knees to the sound of the gym doors opening and closing.

"Everyone, get dressed and join Valentina."

The mat shook and dipped as the others took up their spots next to me. I rose up and twisted my back around, keeping my legs straight.

I heard the door open behind me. "Ah, there you are."

"Sorry I'm late."

I went springing around like a top. Isabella smiled sweetly into Yvette's face.

"Not at all," said Coach. "You're right on time. Get changed and join us."

Isabella headed for the changing rooms, but not before tossing me a shit-eating grin.

Shaking my head, I continued my stretching. *This girl's need to show people up is almost pathological. She should really do something about that.*

I couldn't help but raise my brows when Isabella came back out wearing a blue leotard while the rest of us gathered around in tanks and sweats. Although, come to think of it, I had never seen Isabella in anything so casual—not even jeans.

"I want you all to welcome the newest addition to the team," said Yvette.

I gave a half-hearted clap with the rest.

"Now that everyone is here, we can talk about what I expect for the coming semester." Yvette patted Isabella's back to send her to the line. "We will meet twice a week on Wednesdays and Saturdays."

Isabella's hand shot up. "I can't come on the weekends. I leave campus to practice with my ballet instructor."

"Yes, your... mother was good enough to share the conditions of your being on the team. As I was saying, we meet twice a week and if you miss more than three practices, you are off the team. Our first competition is at the end of October"—excited whispers broke out—"so I expect you all to work as hard as you can." She clapped. "Alright, let's get started."

I was completely focused on practice—I really was. I tried not to spare Isabella a thought, but it wasn't easy.

"Isabella, you're too stiff."

"Isabella, you're thinking too hard."

"Isabella, hip-hop isn't about perfect technique," Yvette said for the third time. I almost felt bad for the ballerina; she looked as frustrated as Yvette sounded. "You don't just master the moves, you own them."

"What is that supposed to mean?" Isabella snapped.

"It means I don't want you to copy me, I want you to add your own personality, okay?" Yvette scanned the sweaty faces until her eyes lit upon me. "Valentina, will you show her, please?"

If I thought Isabella was red before, she was lighting up brighter than Rudolph's nose now. The group fell back as I stepped into the middle of the mat.

To be fair, Yvette's moves were difficult for people who were beginners with hip-hop, but I wasn't one of them. I twisted myself into the spin, and then added a little flip at the end for fun. People were clapping by the time I landed on my feet.

"Very good," Yvette cheered. "See what I mean, Isabella? She did the move, but she wasn't afraid to add her own flair. We're a team of dancers, not robots."

Isabella said nothing. She just went back to the other side of the mat and tried to do the move again. Was I ten kinds of rotten that I had to smother a laugh? It wasn't my fault that she assumed this would be easy. She should have stuck to her pirouettes.

"Alright, everyone, that's it for today," Yvette announced twenty minutes later.

I jogged off the mat over to my backpack. I snagged my water bottle and squirted the lot in my mouth.

"You're pretty good."

I choked. Hacking, I pounded my chest as Eric stepped into my line of sight. "We might win regionals this year with you on the team," he continued like it was no big deal. "No one wants to be on a team with someone marked, but we want to be on a losing team even less. You keep it up and... you're off-limits during practice."

Eric blew off before I could catch my breath to respond. I watched him go with mixed feelings. Knowing that no one was going to purposely drop me on my head, or slick the mat with grease was good of course, but I hated that it depended on me winning for a team that despised me.

Pushing that aside, I gathered my things and made for the door as Isabella slammed out of it. I hopped in the shower right after entering my room and took my time washing practice from my hair and body. Wrapping myself in a fluffy towel, I padded out into my bedroom. My phone buzzed at me from my backpack.

Sofia: I've been looking at photos for over an hour. These are the ones I found that have people wearing red and white masks. Are they here?

The towel almost slipped off, I was rushing so fast to hop on my bed. I pored over every attachment she sent me—zooming in and out, squinting until my eyes hurt—but none of the masks I saw belonged to the person in the woods.

Me: Sorry, they're not there. Were these all you were able to find?

Sofia: Only in the last hour. I've still got more to go, and I think I can get more from Ezra.

Me: Ezra?!?

Sofia: Broadcast club's photographer was going around the party getting in everyone's face. The kid washed out in freshman year, but Ezra may know where the photos are backed up. Goes without saying that I won't bring you up.

Me: I seriously could not do this without you. Thank you, and be careful.

Sofia: I'm not the one actively pissing off the Knights. It's you who should be careful. Love ya.

I shook my head at her last text. Only she could be the perfect mix of supportive and disapproving at the same time.

THE SKY WAS STORMY the next morning. I stuck my head out of the window and could practically drink the moisture in the air.

It's going to piss down in a few minutes. Better get ready.

I closed the window and turned back to my closet. Evergreen expected full uniform whether it was raining, snowing, sleeting, or lava was falling from the skies. I wriggled into my skirt and blazer, then pulled on my bright pink rain boots.

The skies opened just as I was reaching for my umbrella. Quickly, I grabbed the rest of my things and rushed out of the door.

Wind and rain tore at me as I stepped out of the dorm building. I popped open my umbrella and raced across the quad, my shoes squeaking in the soaked grass. I heard screams as those unlucky to be without an umbrella ran for cover, and I pulled mine lower on my face.

My head bent, I saw their feet before I did their faces. I stopped short, yanking up my umbrella as the Knights fanned out and closed me in.

"It was you, wasn't it?" Ryder had to shout to be heard over the rain. In one hand, he was gripping the handle of his umbrella so tightly his knuckles were white.

"Me?" I took a step back and bumped into a solid wall of flesh. I twisted around and found Maverick behind me. "What do you think I did?" They had formed such a tight-knit circle that their umbrellas were giving me extra protection, but only from the rain. The looks on their faces made unease skitter up my spine.

Ezra didn't have his blandly polite smile hanging off his lips today. The fury that wasn't expressed on his handsome face shone brightly in his obsidian eyes. The same couldn't be said for Jaxson or Ryder, their anger was clear in every line of their bodies.

Ryder's lips curled into a snarl. "You leaked those recordings."

"I didn't—"

"Don't fucking lie!" Jaxson burst out. "I thought about it and there's no way I left my phone in class. I had it on me until I went into that broom closet with you."

I shrugged. "That doesn't prove anything. Maybe it slipped out while your pants were down and a custodian got their hands on it."

"This is how you want to play it?" Ryder took a step forward until our umbrellas knocked together. He dropped his and stepped under mine, getting in my face. "A few days ago you were running your mouth about getting us back, and now you don't want to take credit?"

I grinned. "I'm not stupid enough to admit to anything. For all I know Jaxson is taking more secret recordings and he's hoping I'll say it was me so Daddy will forgive him."

Growling, Jaxson lurched forward, but was stopped by Ryder's hand to the chest. "It was you." It was a statement, not a question. "And it was you who destroyed the violin." To my surprise, a faint grin curled his lips. "I've got to give you credit, Val. I said there was nothing you could do, but you proved me wrong. So now, in the spirit of respect, I'll give you one chance to end this now. If one more thing happens—if me or my boys so much as trip over a shoelace—we'll come after you with everything we've got. It'll make last year look like we were playing nice."

Ryder stepped back and the rest of them fell in beside him. He tossed me a wink before turning and leading them through the rain.

I followed at a slower pace. The bell rang while I was halfway up the stairs, but I didn't move faster. Things would get more complicated now but I didn't have regrets. I wanted them to know it was me, and if this meant they would strike, I would only strike back harder.

SOMEHOW I GOT THROUGH my first week of school physically and emotionally intact but the same couldn't be said for Airi, Jaxson, or Isabella. Airi was still weeping over losing her violin, Jaxson was still red from his dad's scolding, and Isabella was still smarting from getting shown up at practice.

The taunts, attacks, and insults against me hadn't stopped for a moment, but it felt good to have left the worst of them bruised.

"I can't believe it was you who destroyed the violin," Sofia said. Saturday practice had let out, but instead of going to the dorms, I wandered around back and joined Sofia on the roof. "Airi is so upset, she's thinking about not auditioning for first chair. I heard her on the phone with her mom arguing about it."

"You did?"

She nodded. "Claire wants to join the orchestra with her flute so I went to watch her."

"Oh. Good for Claire." I wondered if my words sounded clipped to her ears too. Of all the friends who ditched me, I held a particular anger against Claire. We had come from the same place, same neighborhood, and she had joined in with those rich bullies at the drop of a card.

Sofia must have picked up on the need of a subject change. "Are you going to the game tonight?"

"Yeah."

"Really?"

"Yep. I'm going to cheer on the Kings. Show some school spirit."

Sofia made a face. "Right, we'll pretend like I believe that, but seriously, whatever you're going to do, you need to be careful. The first game of the year is a big deal and Lancaster Prep are our rivals. Parents are coming in to see this game, and if there's anything that gets the headmaster's notice, it's embarrassing the school in front of outsiders."

I put my hands up. "I'm not going to embarrass the school. I'm telling you, Sof, I just want to cheer our boys on."

Sofia was quiet for a long time. "You're protecting me, aren't you?"

My grin melted off my face. "Yes," I said, "I am."

"Then it must be bad."

I wanted to tell her it wasn't, but I couldn't. Soon, I excused myself and went to get ready.

Hours later, I was stepping out of my dorm for the game. The headmaster had given special permission for us to be out of our uniforms and I had taken full advantage. I rifled through my closet until I came away with a beautiful white lace dress that fell mid-thigh. I paired it with ivory ankle boots and a white headband decorated with a simple flower.

A few looks came my way as I joined the line of students stomping through rain puddles—nasty looks from the Diamonds in particular. I ignored everyone as I carefully tiptoed around the mud to the football field.

The field's bleachers loomed high in front of us, lit up by luminous beams that almost blocked out the stars. We entered the field and Evergreen students filled in the seats while I hung back.

"Wow," I breathed. I had never been to a football game before, but I had a feeling none of them would have lived up to this anyway. Banners and ribbons in our school colors weaved through the metal of the bleachers, while the blue and yellow of Lancaster Prep dominated on the other side. The energy in the air could almost be felt.

I scanned the faces on our side and picked out many familiar ones. A man that could only be Marcus Beaumont took up two seats in the front row. The guy was as massive as his son. Next to him was a person I recognized from the small screen. Amelia Lennox's charming face lit with a smile at something Marcus said. She looked even nicer and proper than she did on the news. I veered off and went straight for her.

"Mrs. Lennox?"

The older woman turned away and peered curiously at me. "Yes?"

"Hi, I'm sorry to bother you. I just wanted to meet you." I stuck out my hand which she shook. "You're such an inspiration. You built an empire on boldness and integrity and managed to make me *want* to watch the news."

Her laughter was like tinkling bells. "Not easy to do, so that is high praise. So what's your name?"

"My name is Valentina Moon."

"Lovely name." Amelia tugged on my hand and pulled me down next to her. I sat down with a hidden smile as she introduced me to Marcus. "We're here to cheer our sons on," she explained. "Little Ricky is the quarterback and my Ezra is the announcer."

"Little Ricky? Are we talking about the same Maverick?"

Marcus laughed. "Our families have known each other long enough to have seen my son before his growth spurt."

"That's nice."

"Do you know our boys?" Amelia asked.

I nodded. "Yes, we're in the same class."

Amelia beamed. "I hope they don't cause too much of a stir. Of course, we were so proud when we heard they had been chosen as Knights, but I had to keep Ezra out of pictures until his hair grew back."

The adults laughed again while I forced one of my own. Even people grown and living in the real world bought into the strange one that had been created here.

I wonder what she would say if she knew I was marked.

"Yes, that seems harsh. Do they make girls shave their hair too?"

Amelia inclined her head. "They most certainly do. When I went to school here, Cora Daniels had to walk around bald as an egg. I'd have felt for her if she wasn't always harping on me about the length of my skirt." She winked. "I was a bit of a wild child in my younger days."

I joined in on her giggling. It probably wasn't good that I was starting to like her, but one didn't get as far as she did without a winning personality.

Amelia patted my knee. "So tell me more about yourself, Valentina?"

"Okay. I'm from a town called Wakefield and—"

"Mom!" The squishing of rapidly approaching footsteps made me turn my head in time to see Ezra before he was on us. "Mom, what's going on?" He grabbed her arm like he was going to pull her away and narrowed his eyes on me. "Why are you talking to her?"

She frowned. "Excuse me? What do you mean why am I talking to her? Since when are you so rude?"

He pinked. "I just meant—"

"Isn't Valentina a friend of yours?"

I waited as his eyes flicked from me to his mother, then back to me. "Yes," he finally said. In a blink, the mannequin smile was back on his face. "We're real close. I used to tutor her and sometimes we like to mess around. I hope you haven't been listening to her jokes, Mom." His smile grew tight around the edges. "Nothing she says about me is true."

Amelia playfully swatted his shoulder. "We haven't been talking about you, my little narcissist." Amelia suddenly seized her son's face and planted a kiss on his cheek. "I know my baby is an angel."

"Mom," Ezra mumbled, trying to wriggle away. "Everyone is looking."

I didn't bother to smother my laugh.

"Go on." She released him. "The game is starting soon."

"Okay." Ezra let her go and grabbed me instead. "Have fun. I'll give you guys a shout-out. Let's go, Val."

"I—"

I was hauled up and led away as fast as possible. Ezra's hold on my wrist was tight, but not painful. I could have yanked away, but if his mom was still looking, I didn't want it to seem like anything was wrong.

"You seem tense, Ezra," I purred. "Your plastic is cracking."

"Don't know what you're trying to pull, Moon," he hissed. We slipped beneath the bleachers and Ezra spun on me. "What were you doing with my mom?"

I lifted my shoulders. "We were talking about how proud she is of her precious angel. Parents really are the last to know about their kids."

Ezra's dark eyes glittered through the shadows. "You must be some kind of masochist. We warned you what would happen if you tried anything else."

"And that includes a harmless conversation with your mommy? You need to chill, Ezra. Don't be so scared."

A sharp tug on my arm brought me careening into his chest. I didn't let the cry escape as Ezra held me fast. "I'm not scared of you."

His chest was rising and falling almost as fast as mine. Saying he was cracking was a good description. The harsh lines around his eyes, nose, and mouth were the complete opposite of his usual placid smoothness.

Slowly, I extracted my hand and placed it on his chest. I pushed him away firmly. "I'm not going to do anything. I only want a little peek in the announcer's box." I sidestepped him and continued down the tunnel. "Come on. Show me how it's done."

"Wait— You can't just—" Rapid footsteps sounded behind me as Ezra ran to catch up. "You're not going into the box."

I didn't slow my stride. "I thought you weren't afraid of me?"

"I'm not."

"Then you have nothing to worry about."

Ezra stumbled along next to me technically in silence although I could hear his mind moving a mile a minute. If he was trying to figure out what my angle was, he wouldn't.

I led the way to a metal staircase. Behind us, the noise from the field began to fade. It was just us back here.

Eventually Ezra pulled out in front of me and I followed him to a nondescript door with no sign. Ezra pushed inside without bothering to hold it for me and I caught it before it swung shut.

The announcer's box wasn't much to get excited over. It was a simple room with white walls and a fourth that was all windows. Before the windows was a panel of buttons, knobs, chairs, and microphones. Ezra scooted his chair in front of one and I pulled up another.

No words passed between us as we waited for the game to get underway. I looked across the sea of tiny faces hoping to spot Sofia, while at the corner of my eye, Ezra snuck glances at me.

"We know it was you."

I tore my eyes off the field and met his intense gaze. "What?"

"How did you do it?" he went on. "Get into Airi's room and into Jaxson's phone. Airi said a boy went into her room that night. Do you have someone helping you?"

I turned back to the windows. "Don't have a clue what you're talking about."

He scoffed. "Why won't you take credit now? What do you think will happen to you if you admit it that isn't going to happen to you already? Airi is on the warpath. She's talking about suing you no matter what the security camera says."

I shrugged.

"And Jaxson is wrecked. His father says he's never allowed to go into the studio or meet up with the bands again, and it's because of you."

"Me? I thought it was because he stupidly recorded private sessions and then bragged about it to everyone. Lots of people knew he had those songs, I'm not surprised they got leaked."

"*You* leaked them so why would you be surprised."

I responded by flashing him a bland smile.

"I'm guessing you have something *special* planned for me too." Ezra wasn't letting my silence slow him down. "But you can give it up now because it's not going to happen. I changed my passcode this morning just in case. My phone won't be leaving my sight, and you don't have a thing on me and you never will."

I nodded along. "You've thought of everything."

"I did. I get you're upset about being marked, but it was your choice not to drop out when we told you to. You were warned and you received your fate." Ezra leaned forward, his eyes piercing into me. "End this, Moon, you've made your point."

The laughter formed like bubbles and rolled out of my chest in a wave I couldn't stop. "Oh, Ezra," I said between giggles. "I haven't even begun to make my point."

His frown twitched. "You—"

Ring! Ring!

Ezra fished his phone out of his pocket and jammed it to his ear without looking. "What— Oh, right, I— Sorry, sir."

He hung up and scrambled to grab the mic.

I sat back and got comfortable as Ezra slipped into his role. It was funny watching him. Ezra had always thrown me off. I knew what to expect of the other Knights, but this one always seemed like he had more beneath the surface that no one had ever seen. Whoever that was, I suspected he was harder, sharper, but I didn't know if I would ever know for sure. The pleasant, smiling guy before me hid him well.

"Whoo! Our own Maverick Beaumont runs it in for the lead! Call me biased, but the Evergreen Kings are killing it tonight."

He was turned slightly away from me, but that didn't stop me from traveling over the curves and angles of his face.

I wonder what it'll take to meet the real you, plastic man. Maybe... I'll meet him tonight.

I didn't bother to watch the game. What did I know about sports? No, I kept my eyes fixed on Ezra and I hoped it made him uncomfortable. It was a knock at the door that finally made me shift my gaze.

Ezra took off his headphones and stood. "Halftime," he announced.

I didn't know what that was supposed to mean until Ezra walked out of the room and came back with two plates of tacos. My belly grumbled at the sight, suddenly remembering how hungry it was. Ezra didn't look me in the face as he handed one over.

I thought about refusing, but my stomach growled again as though it could hear my thoughts. I accepted the plate without a word and we got down to eating. Silence pressed in on us so thick it felt like a real thing clinging to my skin.

It was a relief when the game resumed and Ezra got back to work.

Soon. It's almost over.

All eyes were on the field, but mine were on the scoreboard. When the clock ran out, everyone cheered the Kings' win, while I privately cheered it finally being over. My eyes scanned the crowd until I found the spot Amelia Lennox had been sitting.

Ezra cut into my thoughts. "You can go now."

"I think I'll stick around," I said simply.

"Why?"

"Why not?"

He shook his head. "Whatever, Moon." He put his back to me and got busy turning things off and putting them away. My eyes were unfocused on him as my attention fixed on something else.

"...so wonderful. Ezra did such a good job."

Amelia's voice echoed through the concrete cavern finding its way to our box. I heard multiple footsteps getting closer, and I got to my feet. I took a deep breath.

"No! Stop!"

Ezra spun around at my scream, just in time to see me race to the opposite side. I placed my hands on the cool plaster, and without pausing to think, reeled back and smashed my face against the wall. The crunch of cartilage breaking filled my ears as blood spurted from my nose.

"What the fuck!" Ezra shouted, nearly as loud as the scream that ripped from my lips.

"Stop!" I stumbled away, scrabbling at the sleeve of my dress.

Riiiippp!

My nails raked deep gashes in my skin as I tore the sleeve away. "Help me! Please!"

I made another run for the wall and strong arms intercepted me. "The fuck is wrong with you?!"

I struggled into Ezra's grasp, bucking against his chest as blood flew from my nose. "Stop! Leave me alone!"

"Val! Sto—"

Bang!

The door flew open, narrowly missing my flailing legs. A pale-faced Amelia stood in the doorway, Marcus just behind her.

"What is going on in here?" she screeched. "Ezra, stop!"

Going limp, I burst into tears.

"Ezra, let her go now!"

"B-but, Mom—"

Amelia darted forward and wrestled me from his grip. "What did you do?!"

I couldn't see Ezra from being buried in her neck.

"Me? Nothing! Mom, I didn't do anything! I swear!"

Amelia twisted around. "Marcus, get her some help."

Hands seized me and lifted me up. I was pressed to a hard chest and carried out as the screaming started. Amelia was nearly unintelligible; her screeching had reached a new pitch. Ezra I could make out. His denials and pleas of innocence echoed through the hall as Marcus carried me away.

Chapter Five

"Miss Moon?" Evergreen's newest doctor poked his head into the nurse's room.

"Yes?"

"Someone is here to see you. I'll send them in."

"Wa—"

The door closed before I could get the word out. I pushed myself up in bed and settled against the pillows. My nose was hurting worse than ever; I needed a top up on the pain meds.

"Val?"

I waved Sofia in. "Hey. Thanks for coming, but what if someone sees you here?"

"I don't care if they do." Sofia rushed in and dragged a stool to my bedside. She gripped my hand. "Val, are you okay? I came as soon as I heard what happened last night." Tears filled her eyes. "I can't believe Ezra did this to you. This is too far."

"Ezra? People know already?"

"Of course they do!" she cried. "Ezra's mom dragged him to the headmaster and told him what he did. There were still some students hanging around the field and they heard everything. Why would he do something like this? Is it because of Jaxson? Do they think it was you? He can't get away with this. I'm going to—"

"Sof, stop." I bit my lip hard, thinking about how much I should tell her.

Tell the truth. Tell someone the truth.

"He didn't do it," I finally said. "He didn't touch me. I did it to myself."

"What?" The hand on mine disappeared. "What are you talking about?"

"I hurt myself, Sofia. Ezra didn't lay a hand on me."

"Then why does everyone think he did?"

"Because that's what I wanted them to think."

She stared at me, completely speechless.

"I know what you're thinking, but I had to do it."

"Had to?" The stool went zipping away as Sofia lurched to her feet. "You had to break your fucking nose!? Val!"

"I know, I know." I grabbed her hand and pulled her down next to me on the bed. The tears were falling now, and they made me feel worse than the aching nose. I didn't want to freak her out, but this had to be done. "This is why I didn't tell you."

"Val, why would you do something like this? How can you not see this is crazy?" She roughly wiped her eyes with the sleeve of her sweater. "I know they hurt you, but this isn't worth it."

"I— Sof, I—" I let in a shuddering breath, and when I let it out, the words tumbled out. "Sofia, before I came here I went through things no one should ever go through. H-horrible, t-terrible things—" My throat threatened to close everything in, but I forced it out. "Things that will always haunt me, but coming here to Evergreen was supposed to be my fresh start. I was going to be safe here. I was going to be happy.

"They took that away. The one thing that I truly wanted was ripped away from me and I had done nothing to deserve it. I don't expect you to understand what I felt when Jaxson told the whole world what my rapist had done to me, but it broke me. Any hope I had shattered into a million pieces, and the only thing that makes me feel right is to make them share my pain."

"Val..." Sofia pressed trembling lips together, not able to go on.

"It's not enough to put a bucket over their doors or stick a 'kick me' sign on their backs. I have to take from them something that matters as much as being here did for me." My eyes slid away from her, staring unfocused at the wall. "Ezra loves his mom and wants to prove himself worthy to take her place. He came after my mom, Sof, so I returned the favor."

"But, Val, you can't— You can't hurt yourself." Sofia grasped my chin and made me face her. "No, I don't know how you feel, but I know how I felt when I heard you had been attacked. I was so scared, and knowing you did that to yourself just freaks me out even more. There has to be a limit."

"I have limits. I—"

"There has to be more," she said firmly. Sofia was steeling under my eyes. "Also, I'm not hearing anymore that you're *protecting* me from your plan. I want to know the whole thing right now, and if I don't like it, we're changing it."

"But, Sof, we can't talk about this here," I protested. "You shouldn't even be here."

"I'm not leaving, and neither are you until you spill it." She folded her arms. "Now."

I thought about arguing some more, but one look at the worry in her eyes made me stop. I had genuinely scared her, and somewhere amidst the darkness, that was reaching me.

I told her about the plan—everything I was going to do to get back at the people on my list. When I was done, Sofia made me come up with a list of rules.

Rules of Revenge

No physical violence against others or myself.
No collateral damage.
No illegal acts.
No sexuality involved.
Know when I've gone too far.
Don't keep secrets.

The last one was for Sofia's benefit and she was pretty adamant about it. I put it in my list and repeated the promise to her about a dozen more times. In the end, she grudgingly accepted my plan, even though it wasn't easy.

"Are you sure about this?" she pressed. "What you want to do to Ryder... I think that comes dangerously close to breaking rule number five, and I mean dangerous. He tried to choke you for getting a B in English, Val. What do you think he'll do if you go through with this?"

I shifted, sinking deeper into the sheets. "I guess I'll find out."

"Maybe there's another way—"

"I know him, Sof." My voice was calm. "Everything rolls off that hard, granite shell. If I want to really get to him, this is the only way to do it, and after everything he's done to me, I still feel he's getting off lightly." I gave her a hard look. "I'm doing this. I won't change my mind."

"Okay, fine. Then... tell me how I can help."

Sofia and I talked a bit more until Dr. Bennett poked his head in and told us I could go. I let her leave ahead of me and then gathered my stuff and left.

It was a bright Saturday morning which meant the hallways were deserted, but the quad was packed. All eyes turned to me when I stepped out onto the grass—including one pair in particular.

Ezra's glare pierced me like a thousand needles through the skin. He stopped with the trash picker hanging over the garbage bag, a remnant from last night's game stuck on the end. For the first time since all this started, the headmaster had been quick with his punishment of the Knights.

I held still as I met his eyes.

I wanted to know the real Ezra, and I have a feeling he is staring back at me right now.

His rage was a palpable thing—reaching across the quad to wrap me tightly like his arms had the night before. Ezra took a step toward me.

"Don't even think about it, Lennox," Coach Panzer snapped. I hadn't even noticed her standing a few feet from him. "Get back to work."

Mumbling something I couldn't hear, Ezra lowered his head and went back to viciously stabbing trash. I looked away from him and realized Panzer wasn't the only one I hadn't noticed. The other Knights sat not far away on a bench near the freshman dorm. Their eyes were fixed on me and I could tell right away they didn't believe Ezra had hurt me. They knew the truth... and they were coming for me.

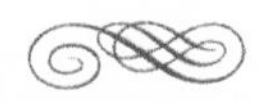

I TURNED AWAY FROM my mirror with a wince. I looked awful. My little button nose had swollen to the size of a grapefruit, and dark purple and blue bruises took up most of my face.

I might have hit that wall a bit too hard, I thought as I sat down at my desk. Sofia could have been right about going too far.

I reached for my phone and tried to take my mind off of it. I had other things to worry about.

The videos from the button cams filled up my phone. I went through every one, edited them, and then sent them off to Alex. The whole process took about an hour and then I finally tackled my homework.

It was midnight by the time I turned out the lights and crawled into bed. The familiar sheets welcomed me and I let myself relax for the first time in over a day. Sleep didn't come quickly, but I lay still in the darkness feeling warm and comfortable.

I'm glad Sofia is with me through this. I might be able to end this sooner than I thought.

I snuggled in deeper and let myself go.

Crash!

"Ahhh!" I sprung up in bed. Frantically, I scrambled for the lamp and almost knocked it over as I turned it on. Light flooded the room, casting its glow over the glass covering my carpet. In the middle of the mess was a large rock.

My sluggish mind tried to make sense of what I was seeing, and my eyes flew to the window just as something else came through. The room lit with another glow as the flaming objects came through the hole in the window, and for one brief second, I saw a gloved hand.

"Hey!" I leaped out of bed. My heart banged in my chest as I raced to the window and yanked it open. I stuck my head out as the figure darted around the corner and disappeared. Everything in me wanted to chase after them, but there was something even more important.

Heat licked at my back and I twisted around. Horror like I had never felt before filled my body at the sight of the fire greedily consuming my rug.

Do something now!

Mind blank with panic, my body moved by instinct to clamber over my dresser and fall onto the pillows. I didn't stop. Scrambling over my sheets, I tipped over the end of my bed and fell hard.

"Fire! Fire!" I got to my feet and raced out the door. "Fire!"

Sprinting, I reached the end of the hall and busted the glass for the fire alarm. The extinguisher hung next to it and I broke it out. Doors opened as I ran back to my room.

"What the fuck is going on?"

I had no time to answer Airi. I burst into my room, pointed the extinguisher, and sprayed wildly—shaky hands and fear making me lose all control. I sprayed long after the fire was out, until firm hands grabbed me.

"Miss Moon, that's enough!" The fire extinguisher was pried out of my grip as I was dragged out of the room. Dazedly, I saw people run into my bedroom as I was taken down the hall and sat on the floor. Gus peered down at me, concern etched into every line of his face. "Are you okay? Did you get hurt?"

He had to repeat his questions a few more times before I could answer. My mind was engulfed with one thought.

Someone tried to kill me. Someone tried to kill me. Someone tried to kill me.

"Miss Moon?"

"I— I'm okay," I rasped. "I didn't get burned."

"What happened?"

I looked into his eyes, and said the only thing I could. "Someone tried to kill me."

"STEP INSIDE, MISS MOON."

Nurse Runyon patted my knee. "Go on, dear. I'll be right out here."

She had been the one they called instead of my mother. To be fair, she had been very sweet and comforting—sitting up with me through the night, getting me my breakfast, and walking with me to the headmaster's office when dawn brought that horrific night to an end.

Sighing, I heaved myself out of the chair and trudged into his office. It was starting to get ridiculous how much time I spent in this room.

"Please have a seat."

I sat down before the headmaster and the head of security. I appreciated the grave looks on their faces. None of them worked too hard at protecting me after getting marked, but at least they took my attempted murder seriously.

Evergreen adopted his steepled-fingered pose. "Miss Moon, the reports I've had from Mr. Cornwallis are disturbing in the extreme. I'm afraid his investigation has supported your fears. Your window was broken from the outside and balls of duct tape were lit on fire and put through your window."

"Duct tape?"

Gus spoke up. "Many don't know that duct tape is flammable. It makes for an easy fire-starter."

I shook my head. "I guess I should have expected a school full of geniuses to get creative."

"I am appalled by this, Miss Moon."

Of course, you are. Can't have anything ruining the reputation of the school.

"I'm told you did not see your attacker?"

"No," I forced out. "I didn't see them. I couldn't even tell you their gender or skin color. I have no clue who it was and I have so many enemies, it could have been anyone."

"It is unfortunate that you did not see them."

My eyes narrowed on Evergreen. I noticed he didn't deny that I had enemies. "What about cameras? Did they pick up anything?"

"The cameras picked up no one entering or leaving their room after curfew," said Gus.

"What do the police say? Have they been called?"

Evergreen's expression did not change. "They have not. This matter will be handled internally."

"What are you talking about? I was almost killed. You have to call the police!" I hadn't acted after I was made to fall down the stairs because I had hoped to use Noemi to root out the Spades. It was different now. They had struck me directly and I was not messing around anymore.

"Mr. Cornwallis and every member of his team are former law enforcement," said Evergreen. "They will conduct an investigation just as thorough as the local police."

"What if I call them myself? And my mother?"

He raised one bushy eyebrow. "I cannot prevent you from doing so, but I'm certain Chief Donaldson will agree with me on this matter. The academy and the Evergreen PD enjoy a close relationship."

I heard the message loud and clear.

"Alright, fine. No police. But what are you going to do to make sure this doesn't happen again? Are you finally going to put cameras outside the dorms?"

"That is not an immediate solution. It would take too long to install them all and connect them to the network, and I'm sure you would prefer not to wait for action." Evergreen took his hands away from his chin and pointed out toward the window. "There is a disused building that was once the staff quarters. In and around the building is outfitted with cameras to discourage students from taking advantage of the empty space. As we speak, the housekeepers are packing up your room and moving your things there."

"Wha— I'm moving?!"

"Yes, you are. Unless you have a better idea for how to prevent future attacks..."

My mouth opened but nothing came out. What was I supposed to say? Sticking more cameras on me may prevent my would-be killer from finishing the job, but it would also make it harder for me to move around and get my revenge.

"No," I forced out. "I don't have a better idea."

He nodded. "Then Mr. Cornwallis will escort you to your new quarters. Have a nice day, Miss Moon."

Just like that, I was dismissed. I followed Gus out and tried to sort through my thoughts as we picked up Nurse Runyon and headed out to the courtyard. It was no good for me to be terrified to go to sleep every night, wondering when the next flaming tape ball would come flying through my window, but even I could see this was a Band-Aid over an amputation. This would not stop the problem, only catching the person behind this would.

But who did it? The Knights? The Diamonds? The faceless Spades?

I had so many people who wanted me gone, and I didn't know who all of them were.

Would Ryder do this as punishment for what I did to Ezra and Jaxson? Is this what he meant by making last year look like he was playing nice?

My brain tried to go there, but no matter how I looked at it, the thought didn't sit right. It's not that I didn't think Ryder could go that far, it's just that I had a feeling that wasn't how he would do it. Ryder wasn't the kind to lurk around in the shadows. If he came for me, he'd do it head-on.

"This is where you will be."

I shook myself out of my musings and laid eyes on the lone building across the courtyard. I had seen it before. It sat starkly next to the main building in full view from the gates of the campus, but Sofia had told me on my first day that it was an empty building and I had no reason to go there.

My eyes swept the three-story red brick structure and spotted multiple cameras just on the face. At least Evergreen had been telling the truth about that. I had no clue if everything else he said about a "thorough investigation" was going to deliver.

Gus produced a key from his pocket and put it in my hand. "This is for the whole building. There are no keypads here as it went out of use before the upgrades, but only you, me, and the headmaster have a key to this place."

"Okay." I took the key from him and stuffed it in my pocket.

"We've put you on the third floor so it'll be tough to throw anything into your room again, but an order has already been put in for shatter-proof glass to be extra safe."

A chill skittered up my spine at the reminder of why all this was necessary. I pulled my jacket tighter around myself. "Thank you."

Gus's ever stern expression broke under his kind smile. "I take your safety very seriously, Miss Moon."

I noticed that he didn't say "we" or "the academy." *He* took my safety seriously.

Maybe I have more allies than I thought.

I nodded and Gus pulled open the door for us to go in. The breath whooshed out of my mouth as I took in what my eyes were seeing. I don't know what I was expecting. Probably cobwebs so thick hanging from the ceiling that I could swing on them like ropes. Rotting floorboards. Ancient furniture that would fall apart if I looked at it too hard. Pretty much everything that came to mind when someone said abandoned building. None of that surrounded me.

Sleek, black hardwood floors spread out beneath my feet. The walls were decorated with paper to match—black and gold and shimmering under the lights of the cobweb-free hanging lamps.

Gus stepped out ahead of me for the staircase and I hurried to keep up with him. Up the steps we went until we hit the top floor and the sound of voices reached me. Half of my possessions were scattered about the hall, and my heart squeezed at seeing the suitcase I had been keeping under my bed. It was unopened, and I hoped it had stayed that way.

There were two doors each on both sides of the hallway and the housekeepers were bringing my things through the door nearest the stairs.

"I don't have to tell you that all dorm rules apply," said Gus. "No boys allowed. In before curfew. No parties. Understood?"

"Sure, no prob..." The word died in my throat as I stepped into my room. The space I had walked into was twice the size of the old dorm. It made my other room look like a gas station men's room.

My head whipped around trying to look at everything at once. The four-poster bed, the walk-in closet, the antique desk, the sitting area—an actual sitting area, like I would be having my one friend over to sip tea and cookies on that couch.

"I hope this will do," Gus continued. "I know you would rather be with your friends, but this is the best solution I could come up with."

"Oh, it'll do," I breathed. I had no love for the sack of shit that tried to burn me alive, but I couldn't deny they had gotten me an upgrade. "Thank you," I said to the staff in the middle of hanging up my clothes. "I can take it from here."

"Are you sure?" said one of the housekeepers. "You've been through a lot. We're more than happy to help."

"I appreciate that, but I'm fine now."

I had to repeat that about a half dozen times before they would leave. When I was finally alone, I set about the task of fixing up my room. The whole thing took so long, and was made longer by Sofia's constant stream of worried text messages. Between unpacking and reassuring her, I missed lunch and was forced to eat a bag of chips I had stashed away from home. I breathed a sigh of relief when I put away my last bottle of Honey Hair shampoo.

I left my massive bathroom and threw myself in bed. My phone buzzed moments after I hit the pillow.

Alex: It's ready.

That blew away all thoughts of sleep. I quickly typed a reply.

Me: What are you going to do?

Alex: Nothing I haven't done before. All you need to do is tell me when you're ready to pull the trigger.

Me: Not now. Tomorrow. 12:15 exactly.

Alex: You got it.

I tossed my phone next to me and fell back into the sheets. What happened last night hadn't changed what I needed to do. There was another name that would be crossed off my list.

I DIDN'T HAVE THE USUAL eyes following me across the quad the next morning. Instead, I made a quiet trek through the front courtyard and slipped onto the first floor. The stares didn't hit me until I stepped onto the second. Whispers followed me as I walked to my locker.

"Did you hear what happened?"

"Someone tried to kill her."

"I know she's marked, but what kind of psycho would do this?"

"I'm not having anything to do with murder."

"This is getting crazy."

My ears were perked and listening closely. This was the first time since that damn card showed up in my locker that my classmates were whispering something about me that I wanted to hear.

Yes, you stupid little sheep. Realize that what is happening to me is wrong.

I rounded the corner and stopped dead. A single person leaned against my locker, clearly waiting for me. I held still for one more second, then kept walking.

"Morning, Ryder," I said lightly. "What brings you here? Come to threaten me? Choke me? 'Cause you should know I've been growing my nails extra long in case I need to rake them across your face again." I wiggled my fingers between us for effect.

Ryder laughed. His hand closed around mine before I could pull away. "No one's going to hurt you, Val." His thumb glided over the sensitive skin of my palm and I couldn't stop the shiver that traveled up my hand and through my body. I yanked my hand away. "I'm just here to talk," he continued. "Ezra told me the truth of what happened in the announcer's box." His eyes swept over my bandaged nose. "You should know he only got a few weeks of trash duty and a month of Saturday detention. If you thought this was going to get him kicked out, you were wrong."

I shrugged. "I'm not surprised one of the precious Knights gets away with hurting me."

"He didn't touch you."

"Of course you would believe that."

"Believe that you're damaged enough to break your own nose?" A smirk curled his lips. "Yeah, I believe that. You forget how well I know you."

"I know you too, Ryder," I replied as I gave him a smile to match. "And I'm not the only one who's damaged. In my case, I know why. But you... I've never understood what made you so broken." I took a step back. "Maybe it would help if you talked to your dad about it."

His face twisted into the familiar frown. "Not likely to do that as the guy has been fucking missing for over a year."

I cocked my head, giving him a strange look. "No, didn't you hear me? I said to talk to your dad."

His frown deepened. "What's that supposed to mean?"

"Gotta go. Time for homeroom."

"Hey!"

I ignored him and continued on my way. I'd have to get my books later.

Homeroom was packed by the time I walked in. Almost everyone was there including Ezra. His face was expressionless as he tracked me across the room to the phone box, but as always, his eyes said more. I put my phone away and headed for my seat.

"Hold on, Miss Moon." Wheeldon's voice stopped me halfway. "I've changed your seat. You'll be in the front row now."

I turned around and went to the desk he pointed at. Probably a good call to move me away from Ezra, fake beating or not. I sat at my desk with nothing to do but try to ignore the whispers around me. I wasn't naïve enough to think the fire would make my class lay off, but many of them looked genuinely freaked out. Maybe I could use that to root out who only wanted me gone, and who wanted me dead.

Homeroom let out and I hurried to my locker to get my textbooks. It was nearly impossible to focus on schoolwork that day, and if my professors noticed me wandering, they cut me some slack. Every time I looked at the faces around me, I saw that gloved hand and a dark figure escaping into the night.

The bell chimed for lunch and a chorus of zippers, snapping textbooks, and chairs scraping the floor broke into my thoughts. I got up and joined the crowd on the way to the cafeteria. The lunch lady handed me a tray of chicken cobb salad and pita bread pizza and I took it to my spot at the window. With one eye, I focused on my food, but the other was fixed on the clock.

12:04

12:08

My nails dug into my palms as the seconds ticked down.

12:15

Not bothering to hide my smile, I picked up my pizza and tore off a bite.

"THAT IS REALLY COMING along, Valentina."

I looked up from my misshapen hunk of clay to shoot Scarlett a look. "Really? Because I'm not even sure what it is."

Scarlett threw her head back laughing. She once offered to let me hang out in her class when I needed a break and today, I decided to take her up on it. The second my last class let out; I came straight to the art room. Really, I was just delaying the fireworks, but it was nice sitting in this colorful space messing around with clay.

"I'm glad you joined me today, Val." Scarlett borrowed a stool from another workstation and sat next to me. I caught the serious expression dawning on her freckled face and bit back a sigh. So much for ignoring my troubles. "How have you been, Val? I heard about what happened with you and Ezra. Not to mention the fire in your room."

"I won't lie." I pressed my thumb into the mound of soft clay, dotting it with holes. "It's been a rough few days."

"I'll bet. Your nose. Is it broken?"

I nodded.

Scarlett sucked in a breath. "I can't believe Ezra would do this. He was such a sweet boy."

I said nothing.

"And the fire. Who would do something like this?"

"Seems like the kind of thing that would happen in a place that allows kids to be targeted and tortured." The words fell from my lips unbidden. "I mean, if I could be tripped down the stairs and have my medical history blasted to the world, why shouldn't I be lit on fire too. It's just the life of the marked."

"Valentina..."

I took my eyes off the mess I was making and met hers. She held my gaze for all of five seconds and then looked away. "Is this the part where you pretend you don't know what I'm talking about?" I asked. "Like all the other staff do."

"No," she said softly. "This is the part where I tell you the harsh truth. Our—my—acknowledgment will not help you. There is nothing I can do."

"I don't understand that," I burst out. "Why does everyone in charge act like they are so helpless? It's fucking Lord of the Flies in here!"

Scarlett didn't scold me for my language. Instead, she rested her hand on my arm and squeezed. "In that book, there was something at play bigger than those boys could fight. It's the same here. Evergreen has been this way long before you and I arrived and it will remain long after. There are people at work to make it so."

"The Spades," I whispered.

Scarlett nodded. Once.

"So they just get to run around the school, doing whatever they want, and no one stops them."

"*You* can stop this, Val. You don't have to put up with this. There are so many good schools."

I was shaking my head before she finished. "I'm not leaving. There are many *good* schools, but this one is the best. I'm not giving this chance up."

I expected more arguing, fussing, groans of frustration, maybe a few headshakes, but instead she smiled. "You're a brave girl, Valentina. Much braver than I would have been and... braver than I am now." Lowering her head, Scarlett took a deep breath. "You deserve more than 'there's nothing I can do.' I don't know how yet, but I'm going to find a way to help you. Put a stop to this."

Something I hadn't allowed myself to feel for a long time began to blossom in my chest. "Really? You mean that?"

Scarlett straightened. "Yes. Just tell me what I can do."

"I mean, I— I don't—" I bit my lip, thinking. There was one thing I really wanted to know. "Walter McMillian."

She blinked. "McMillian?"

"Yes." I got the rest out before I could stop myself. "I want to know more about what happened to him, but I can't find so much as his name online and people don't tell me much these days. Do you know anything about what happened to him?"

Scarlett opened her mouth.

"I know it's a longshot," I blurted. "You probably weren't born when he went to school here."

"I wasn't, and thank you for noticing." Scarlett's grin lightened the mood. "I admit I don't know much about Walter, but..." A funny look came over her face. "Hang on one second."

That was all the warning I got before Scarlett popped out of her seat and hurried across the room. Behind her desk was her personal supply closet. She ducked inside. "I wasn't here," she called back to me, "but my father was. He was two years ahead of Walter, and you know they keep the classes separate, but I asked him once what he knew about what happened."

Scarlett reemerged and this time she was holding a book. She held it up triumphantly. "This is his yearbook. Borrowed it once to surprise him with a portrait of his younger days."

I sat up so fast I almost toppled off the stool. Seriously? Scarlett had been sitting on this the whole time. She flipped through until—

"Ah ha. Here he is." She placed the book in front of me and pointed to a singular face at the bottom of the page. "Walter McMillian."

After a year of thinking about this guy and who he was, there he was smiling back at me. I reached for the book, then stopped when I saw my brown hands.

He was cute.

Not sure why that was my first thought, but I couldn't help it. Even with the long poofy hair and oversized glasses, Walter had the strong jaw and classically handsome looks that made people swoon.

"So he was a sophomore," I said, peeking the yellow blazer.

"That's right. That's when it all went down, I hear."

"Someone told me his friend was marked and he tried to help them."

"Not just his friend." Scarlett pulled the book back toward her and flipped through again. "It was his girlfriend. He loved her, and refused to turn on her." Scarlett pushed it back and pointed to another face. "It's a shame. His intentions were good."

I gazed at the lovely face that looked back at me. No wonder Walter couldn't let her go. Not even those ridiculous hairstyles could cover up how beautiful this girl was. It wasn't just her features, but the sweetness you could see in her smile. I couldn't imagine anyone wanting to hurt her.

"Nora Wheatly," I read. "Do you know what happened to her? Why she was marked?"

I deflated when she shook her head. "I know she left the school after he died, but Father wouldn't give me more details. It was a dark time that hit the school hard. Applications dropped to double digits, and students jumped at their own shadows. No one wants to think about what was done to Walter, or the fact that his killer was never caught."

I shivered. I couldn't blame them. This stuff was frightening. "It's not right what happened to him," I whispered. "To both of them."

"No, it wasn't." Scarlett closed the yearbook. "But we can't change it. All we can do is make sure it never happens again."

To me, went unsaid.

MY THOUGHTS WERE HEAVY as I left Scarlett's classroom. *I haven't really learned anything new, but at least I know their names.*

Sighing, I pushed Walter from my thoughts for the time being and rescued my phone from homeroom. It buzzed in my hand the second I grabbed it.

I hid a grin as I walked past Wheeldon's desk. *Cue the fireworks.*

Sofia: Val, the dorm is blowing up.

Sofia: I wish you were in the group chat so you could see this.

Sofia: Screw this. I'm sending you screenshots.

I scrolled through the avalanche of photos she sent me as I let myself into my new building. It was even better than I thought.

Taking the stairs two at a time, I raced to my room, burst inside, and yanked open my laptop. I logged on to my newsfeed and drank in the trending stories.

"Evergreen Gone Wild."

"What Really Goes On In The World's Top Prep School?"

"Evergreen Students Involved With Prostitution?"

"Bullying At Evergreen?"

It was so beautiful I thought I would cry. I picked a new site at random and was taken to another page. I didn't bother to read the article; I only had eyes for the video.

Alex had done an amazing job piecing together the footage from my button cam. He took hours of bullying, taunts, insults, secrets, and stairwell hookups and condensed them down to a five-minute movie trailer of what life in Evergreen was really like—for me.

I had gotten lucky with the hookup video. After a few nights of sticking my head in the stairwell on the way to my room, I finally overheard the sounds that could not be mistaken. A quick run upstairs, ducking my head like I was oh so embarrassed, and the button got the cherry on top of what was a shocking video.

"I was thinking five— No, four dollars for a fuck."

"There are pills that will help you stay awake to study. You can have some of mine. I also have coke if you're really hard up."

"Can I borrow your razor? I'm sneaking Jared in through the window tonight."

"Cade is going to beat me out for valedictorian at this rate. I'm thinking I should just cheat. There's a junior who sells term papers for only five hundred a pop."

"Stop playing hard to get. Give it up already, slut."

"Out of the way, bitch."

"Why couldn't that fall down the stairs have finished you off?"

That last gem Natalie shouted at me across the cafeteria. I had gotten it all, but thanks to Alex, my voice and anything else that could point to me had been scrubbed from the video before they sent it off.

I picked up my phone again and opened the messages from Alex.

Alex: The video is up. Hope you're pleased with the results.

I thought of the pages of accusations, curses, threats, and blubbing from the group chat, and could just imagine the look on Evergreen's face as he fell under the wave of bad press and angry phone calls.

Rule Number One, I remembered. *Evergreen values its reputation above all.*

I typed my reply.

Me: More than pleased.

<u>The List</u>

~~Airi Tanaka~~

Natalie Bard

Isabella Bruno

Maverick Beaumont

~~Ezra Lennox~~

~~Jaxson Van Zandt~~

Ryder Shea

The Spades

~~Evergreen Academy~~

Chapter Six

"It was her, wasn't it?"

"Of course, it was her. Who else would do something like this?"

"But Valentina wasn't there when I said that about the pills." The whispering has started up again, but I was surprised to hear it was mixed. Plenty of people were blaming me, but not all were, thanks to me leaving my cam in the locker room more than once. I had heard so many juicy things in there while I was around, that I knew my cam would pick up even more when I wasn't.

"My mom recognized my voice," I overheard Darren say. "Saying that I would pay four dollars for a fuck. She tore into me for half the night."

"I think it was Katie Reynolds." These murmurings came to me while I was spinning my dial. "She got into it with Natalie at the start of school and said people were going to see what she was really like."

"Shit," another voice said. I kept my face forward, not wanting them to know I was eavesdropping. "No one likes the Diamonds, but you can't go around doing things like this. Evergreen is going to go mad."

Hmm. No one likes the Diamonds? That's good to know.

I got my things out and headed to homeroom. I stepped inside and realized right away that something was wrong. Wheeldon was up and glaring at the four boys standing in front of the phone box.

A hush fell on the classroom as I approached the Knights. "Excuse me."

Ryder held out his hand. "Give us the phone, Moon."

"Why would I do that?"

"We know you leaked that video to the press," said Ezra.

"And when we get proof," Jaxson continued, "you're out."

Ryder stepped forward. "Give me the phone."

I peered over my shoulder at Wheeldon. "Aren't you going to do something about this?"

"I... can't." His grimace showed how hard he was fighting with himself. "The headmaster told me not to interfere. You need to give them the phone."

Sighing, I didn't fight it anymore and plucked it out of my backpack.

"Unlock it."

"A please wouldn't kill you," I mumbled to Ryder as I pressed my thumb to the pad. The home screen lit up and I put my cell in his outstretched hands.

Ryder lifted it over his shoulder and Maverick took it. No one uttered a sound as Maverick went through my cell. I didn't watch him; my eyes were fixed on Ryder's fathomless silver pools. Was this how it was always going to be? Us on opposite sides? Always facing off?

Ryder spoke without breaking our gaze. "What did you find, Rick?"

"Nothing."

"What?" That made him look away. Ryder pivoted to face his friend. "What do you mean nothing?"

"There's nothing here, man. The only video is of a kid smearing avocado on his face. The texts are to her mom. There's nothing else."

I smiled wide, showing off all of my teeth. "See. I told you."

Ryder flashed me a look over his shoulder. "She must have erased it."

"There are ways to find out."

"Then do it!"

Maverick's expression was calm as he pocketed my phone. "Let's go then. I need my computer."

The taller boy walked around us and made for the door. Ryder grabbed my hand. "You're coming with us."

"I've been walking without help since I was a toddler." I wrenched my wrist out of his grip. "I've got this."

I followed Maverick out and the five of us made a tense line through the hall. Maverick, then me, Ryder, Ezra, and Jaxson silently trekked to a room I had been in many times before.

Maverick pushed through into the Knights' room and went straight for his laptop. I came in at a slower pace. It looked the same as I remembered. Metal bits and gadgets on the coffee table for Maverick. Records for Jaxson. Ryder's piano taking up an entire corner. And the cleanliness of the room reflecting Ezra's perfectionism.

I broke away from the group and wandered around.

"Sit down," Ryder snapped.

"No, thanks."

My feet took me to Jaxson's record collection and I didn't give a thought to pulling one out. *Wow, he's gotten even more since I've last been in here. I would kill for—*

A hand appeared in my line of vision and plucked the record from my fingertips. "No one touches my records." Jaxson's breath ghosted over my ear and I was sharply reminded of his naked body pressed to my back while he nibbled on me. "Not even you, baby."

A flush went up my neck. "You're back to calling me baby? Does that mean something?"

Jaxson's answer was to put his hands on my waist and spin me around. I let him march me to the couch and sit me down next to Maverick.

Ezra sat across from me, eyes fixed, but saying nothing. I wondered when he was going to confront me about what happened after the game. I also wondered if it was a bad sign that he hadn't already.

"Have you found something yet?" Ryder demanded. He wasn't sitting. He had taken up a spot leaning against his piano.

Maverick didn't answer as he plugged my phone into his laptop and got to work. He seemed immune to Ryder's mercurial nature like no one I had ever seen before. Even the friends of Ryder that I had met when we were little were afraid of that guy.

"You're not going to find anything," I piped up. "I had nothing to do with that video."

"Like you had nothing to do with leaking the audio files, breaking the violin, and faking a beating from Ezra?" Ryder taunted.

I smiled at him. "How am I supposed to have done it anyway? My phone stays locked up same as everyone, and this whole thing started blowing up in the middle of the school day." I crossed my legs and leaned back into the cushions. "I'd also like to point out I'm not the only one who'd want to strike back at this place."

"Maybe not," said Ryder, "but you're the only one who said out loud that you would do it."

I shrugged. "I say a lot of things. *You* have to prove that I did those things, and I'm not hearing from anyone how I used my phone to record people when it was locked all day with Wheeldon."

"Button cam."

Two whispered words from Maverick and I went rigid. My attention darted to the back of his head. *It's not enough for him to be a hulking mass of muscles and good looks, but the bastard has to be smart too?*

What did you expect? another voice countered. *You learned about the button cams from him.*

Ryder straightened up. "What did you say, Rick?"

I held my breath.

"I said there's nothing," he answered. Maverick turned the laptop around. "You can see for yourself. The card hasn't been wiped. She doesn't have the video."

This would have been time to give Ryder a triumphant smile, but I didn't take my eyes off of Maverick. What was he doing?

"Then someone is helping her." Frustration laced Ryder's voice. "It must be that guy Airi told us about."

"All these texts are harmless, even the deleted ones. She doesn't talk about us."

Ryder didn't seem to have heard him. "Give it up, Val. Who is it?"

I shook my head. "No clue who you're talking about."

Jaxson pressed in closer to me. His hand was gentle as he stroked my cheek. "Maybe if we ask nicely, she'll tell us."

"Be careful," I returned. "I bite."

"It could be one of her old friends," Ezra spoke up. "They could be pretending they split with her, but the whole time have been helping her strike against us."

"Now that"—Ryder moved to tower over us—"would be a big mistake."

I did not like where this conversation was going. I couldn't have them looking at Sofia. She was sweet. Sweet as in if she ever went through the things I have, she wouldn't survive it. I would not let them hurt her.

"But it was a white guy on the camera," Jaxson reminded. "Which means it couldn't have been Eric Eden, and he was the only guy she hung around with."

I scoffed. "It's creepy to know how much you guys kept tabs on me and my old friends, but thanks to your buddies, the Spades, old is what they are." I got to my feet. "You've kidnapped me from class, broke into my phone, violated my privacy, and you still haven't found what you're looking for. Is that enough for one day or do you have more?"

Ryder's eyes were cold as they looked me up and down. "It looks like you win this round, Val, but I do have one more question. How are you going to do it? Get back at me and Maverick?"

I snatched up my phone and turned to go. "Now that would be telling, wouldn't it?"

"There's nothing you can do against us."

"Ezra said the same thing."

A furious hiss to my right told me what Ezra thought about that. I tossed him a wink on my way to the door.

"I'm actually looking forward to it."

I paused with my hand on the knob.

"Whatever it is you have planned for me," Ryder continued. His smooth voice floated over the heads of the other guys and caressed my ear. "It'll be fun to watch your stupid plan fall apart. There is not a single thing you can do that will affect me. How long before it's my turn, Moon?"

Slowly, I turned my head and peered at him over my shoulder. "But, Ryder... I've already started." I smiled. "Did you have that talk with your dad yet?"

I was out the door before he could find a response.

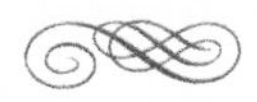

IN THE WEEKS THAT FOLLOWED, life at Evergreen had fallen into a new normal—if that was the word that could be used.

Rumors still ran hot and heavy, but although no one knew for sure, many thought I was the one that leaked the video, and because of it, the bullying eased up by so much it was like the mark had been lifted, but the punishments that came down for everyone else in the aftermath of the leaked video were of biblical proportions.

The implication of drugs, prostitution, cheating, and bullying running rampant in the school kicked off more bad press than I thought. Evergreen was trending on national news for weeks. People lapped up the notion that the "best school in the world" was just another seedy crap pile for the rich and privileged.

The public demanded a closer look at what really went on in Evergreen, and despite how hard I know he must have tried, Evergreen wasn't able to stop the investigation that was launched against the school. Students were never so well behaved as when police were crawling all over the campus with sniffer dogs, or when we were all brought in separate rooms and questioned about the prostitution.

A few voices from the videos were picked out by their parents, and they wielded the long arm of their displeasure through the walls of the campus. The girl who talked about the coke was pulled out of school. The kid who wanted to cheat to beat Cade was easy to find as number two in our class, and she cracked like an egg when her mother came bursting into campus. She gave up the junior handing out term papers and both were gone in a week.

Then there was Evergreen himself. Someone said he would go mad, but Evergreen blew way past mad and fell into a towering rage that was a sight to behold. The broadcast the day after the investigation ended was explosive.

"Never in all my days have I seen such a disgusting display!" he had roared. "The shame you all have brought upon this school is— A shining reputation that has lasted for over a hundred years destroyed in a—" The man was so worked up he couldn't finish sentences. "If I ever find out who released that video!" His bellow had made his microphone screech and I winced for more than one reason.

"Canceled!" he shouted. "Everything canceled! No clubs! No dances! No breaks!" He smashed his hand on the desk. "No *food*! Detention for every—!"

It was at that point the video had been cut off so the headmaster could have a chance to cool down. The next day when he gathered us in the auditorium to try again... he was even more unreasonable.

The rest of the staff hustled him off the stage, and it was another week before we were pulled out of class and brought into the auditorium once more.

Evergreen cleared his throat. "Hello, sophomore class." His eyes were fixed on the podium and the speech he had written down.

"I will tell you what I have told the freshman class, and what I will go on to tell the juniors and seniors.

"The embarrassment that has been brought upon this school in the wake of the video is unacceptable and cannot go unaddressed. The party or parties involved have not come forward, as such, these consequences will apply to all of you. All club activities are canceled for the rest of the semester. This includes sports."

The shouts that went up were quickly silenced by a harsh look from the headmaster.

"Unless it is academic in nature, it is canceled," he continued. "The soda machines that were once a school treat will be removed. Cameras will now be installed in the dorm stairwells and students are not allowed to be in the locker rooms without staff present. I have also instituted new rules and policies that are effective immediately.

"Phones, cameras, and any recording devices are now banned from Evergreen campus."

If I thought the reaction to losing club activities was bad, it was nothing compared to the chaos that erupted after he said that. It took over ten minutes for the staff to quiet the room down for Evergreen to keep going, and when he did, it was to glares that would have lit his salt-and-pepper hair aflame.

"A phone is a privilege," he went on, "not a right, and you all have lost that privilege. From now on, there will be a designated landline in administration for you all to speak to family and friends outside of campus. Then there are your laptops..."

I couldn't be sure, but it seemed like Evergreen had been enjoying it.

"All laptops will be confiscated, and in return, you will receive school-issued laptops to complete your work. These computers will be connected to the school network and closely monitored. To make sure no attempts are made to get around these rules, luggage will now be checked upon entering campus after breaks.

"As for policies that have not changed, but it's clear you all need to be reminded of, cheating or being caught in possession of drugs is an automatic expulsion from this school." Evergreen glanced up from his cards and pierced the audience with a look. "I trust we will never have a situation like this again."

That had been October. Now we were approaching the end of November and Evergreen had more than made good on his threats. The phones and laptops had been taken away, and all the clubs, including dance, had been canceled for the semester.

I had been lucky enough to get a message to Alex who sent a virus that wiped everything from my laptop. It wasn't fun to lose everything again, but I wasn't taking chances. As for the phone, I got around that the same way I fooled Maverick. I had two.

Two phones. Two sim cards. Both identical.

I had done everything on my regular phone, but after the video went live, I busted out the one I had been using to talk to Mom and Adam. That was the one I placed in Evergreen's waiting hands.

Even though I escaped that unscathed, the changes hit me too. There was no more texting Sofia. No more dancing. No more messing around on my laptop. That students were now tiptoeing around me in fear that I was hiding a few more recording devices wasn't so bad, but I could have done without the rest.

"I knew he would be mad, but I wasn't ready for this." Sofia set her tray down on the table. We were up in our spot having breakfast. It was the only way we got to hang out nowadays, and we were careful to mix it up so people didn't notice us missing.

I handed her my strawberry cup before she could steal it. She had been on a sweetness binge since they took our only treat from us: the soda machine.

"Madame Madeline is livid," she said around a mouth full of strawberry. "She said 'how dare they treat my daughter like a prisoner.' She actually called a lawyer. Can you believe it?"

I snorted. "I can believe it. Olivia was spitting. I told her everything over the administration phone and she demanded I put Evergreen on the line. I don't know what she said to him, but he went redder than a maraschino cherry."

"I hope she tore him a new asshole. He took away everything that makes Evergreen bearable. I almost feel bad for approving this plan."

"We didn't make Evergreen do these things. And maybe if he cared as much about this school *actually* being a better place as he does about it appearing like one, then we wouldn't be in this mess."

She heaved a sigh. "Let's not talk about this anymore. Finals are coming up and then we'll be free of this place. Tell me you're coming to stay again."

"I can't. I've been away from Adam for so long, and I think your mom might develop a permanent wrinkle between her brows if I show up with a baby again."

"Goodness. You know, I don't think other big sisters love their brothers as much as you do."

I just smiled. "None of them are as cute as him."

"I can't argue with that." Sofia leaned in and snuggled into my side. "Would your mom mind if I came to stay with you?"

"No way. It would be amazing if you came over again. We had so much fun last year."

"Yay. Then it's settled."

"Will Madeline keep our secret? It would be a disaster if people here found out where you went."

"She won't tell. I'll make sure of it."

We talked for a little more and then I said I had to go. Finals were coming up and this year was no less hard than the first. I was heading back to my room to get my textbooks and then I was spending this beautiful November Saturday in the library.

I passed lounging couples on the quad and slipped into the main building. The hallway was hushed; the only sounds breaking the silence were my soft footfalls. I pushed through the double doors and stepped into the courtyard.

Pausing on the cobblestones, I filled my lungs with crisp air. I loved it out here. Everyone hung out in the quad so I had this space to myself to listen to the cackling crows and the bubbling of the fountain. Somedays I liked to bring out a blanket and study out here.

Maybe I'll do that today instead of going to the library. Can't let this go to—

"Valentina! Look out!"

My head whipped around just as a streak tackled me.

Crash!

I screamed as we fell to the ground in a tangle of limbs. They came down on me hard, punching the air from my lungs as something showered us.

"Shit. Are you okay?!"

I couldn't speak. I struggled to catch my breath as the person climbed off of me and came into focus. Jaxson's golden locks brushed my forehead as he bent over me. "I'm sorry. I didn't mean to hit you so hard."

Jaxson straightened, and all of a sudden, I was rising with him. He lifted me into his arms and cradled me to his chest. From my position, I got a look at the planter that crashed into the spot I had just been standing in. The breath left my lungs again for an entirely different reason.

"Come on. We need to get out of here."

Jaxson stuck his head out of the overhang, scanning above him, then he took off with me in his arms. If my mind hadn't gone white with panic, I might have stopped him but the only thing I could register was the sickly shiver that started in my spine and was spreading through the rest of my body.

I would have died if he hadn't saved me.

Jaxson ran all the way to my building. "Valentina, where's the key? We need to get inside."

I tried to reach for my pocket but my hand was shaking too much to go inside.

"It's okay. I got it."

Jaxson put me on my feet and I stumbled. He caught me before my legs could give out. Holding me up with one hand, he used the other to get my key and let us inside. Jaxson firmly shut and locked the door, and then I was in his arms again.

"Wait..." I managed.

He didn't slow down. Jaxson bounded up the stairs and made for my room without me having to tell him where to go.

I was trembling worse than ever as he let himself inside and crossed the room to my bed. He gently placed me down and pulled the covers to my chin.

"You should be safe here. I'll go—"

Jaxson made to get up but my hand flashed out of the blanket. I gripped him so tightly he cringed at the nails digging half-moons into his wrist.

"D-d-don't—" I gasped. The band around my chest was tightening; I felt like I would never breathe again.

"Alright, I get it." Jaxson grabbed my hand and extracted his wrist from my clutches. "I'm not going anywhere."

He said that, but when he stood again, my heart squeezed. "N-no."

Jaxson continued what he was doing. He toed off his sneakers, and my mattress dipped as he climbed up and settled down next to me. Jaxson stayed above the covers, but that didn't stop me from feeling his heat as he pulled me to him and draped one arm over my waist. The other stroked my hair, brushing it back the way I would never tell him I loved.

I didn't know how long we lay there, but no words passed between us as the light from my window dimmed to a dusky orange. Slowly, my racing heart eased back into its normal rhythm and my shakes went away.

Still, it was a long time before I trusted myself to speak.

"Jaxson?"

"Yes?" His lips were right next to my ear, and his breath on the back of my neck made goose bumps erupt on my skin. I was highly aware of the fact I was cuddling with my enemy in an empty building.

"Did you... see who it was?"

"No." His finger was still playing in my hair. It was highly distracting. "I saw that thing coming for you and reacted. I didn't look up."

"I would have died," I whispered. "I'm always in the courtyard alone. If you hadn't seen—" A realization came crashing through my mind. "Hang on. What the hell were you doing there anyway? I'm always there *alone*."

I felt his shrug against my back. "You're going to be pissed, but keep in mind I saved your life. You've got Ryder and Ricky jumpy about what you're going to do next. Ryder doesn't like how quiet you've been so he told me to follow you around."

"What?!" I sprang up, knocking his hand off me. "You've been stalking me?! For how long?!"

Jaxson put his arms behind his head and fell onto his back. He looked totally comfortable in my bed. "Only a few days, but like I said, it's because of that I saved your life, so you're not allowed to be mad at me."

"You wanna bet?" I pointed at the door. "Get out."

"Why?" His grin was wicked. "I thought we were spooning, baby."

My cheeks were on fire. I couldn't believe this asshole.

"I'm glad I was there," he went on. The smirk faded. "That could have been really bad, Valentina."

I swallowed hard. "I know... Thank you."

"We don't want you dead," he replied. "Not even Ryder."

Jaxson tugged on one of my folded arms and pulled me down. I didn't let myself think as he rested my head over his heart. It *thump, thump, thumped* in my ear while he put his arms around me once more.

"Are you feeling better?"

"Yes," I mumbled. The heat was spreading from my cheeks and zinging through my veins. I had no idea what the hell I was doing. I had even less of a clue about what he was doing. "Why are you being so nice to me?"

"It's what happens when we reach the point in the relationship when you've seen me naked." Jaxson must have been burning up because I was hotter than a stove now. "Just wait and see how nice I'll be when I see *you* naked."

"You're not going to see me naked," I retorted automatically.

"Bet you thought I'd never end up in your bed either, and look at us now."

"How can you make jokes, Jaxson? I know you hate me for leaking those songs."

Jaxson stilled. "So you're finally done pretending it wasn't you?"

"We both know it was me so why pretend? I did it, and I would do it again. Stop acting like you're not pissed."

"I wasn't pissed. I was fucking out-of-my-mind raging after what you did to me. My dad banned me from the studio and has barely taken my calls since the songs got out. Also, Interstellar Records is in some serious legal shit. I wanted to get back at you and hard."

The stupidity of allowing this guy to be alone with me would have been hitting me if it wasn't for something he kept saying. "Why are you talking in past tense?"

"Because I realized sometime around you breaking your own damn nose... that you must be feeling the same thing. We— I did some really awful shit to you. I went way too far, and honestly, you let me off easy."

I couldn't believe what he was saying. Did he really mean it? "Jaxson, if this is some kind of trick—"

"It's not a trick. I don't know about the other guys, but it's over for me. I hit you hard; you struck back. We're even." His arm tightened around me. "If you don't believe me, then think about the fact that I know you've been hanging with my girl Sofia in some secret rooftop hideout and I haven't told Ryder."

I snapped my head up. "Oh no, Jaxson, you can't say anything! If people come after her—"

"I'm not going to tell anyone. I'm tired of hurting you, Val, especially when I don't know why I have to."

My chin sank back on his chest. "I'm not sure what to do with this."

"Do you still want revenge against me?"

"No," I admitted. "I'm done."

"And I'm done too. So let's just start there."

I didn't reply. I didn't know how to.

"Besides," he began, "we have bigger problems. Whoever is after you isn't playing around. What if the next time, I'm not there?"

"I don't know."

"What happened to the bodyguard?"

"I couldn't trust her."

"Then find one you can."

I peered at him. "You're not going to tell me to drop out?"

"I might if I thought for a second your stubborn ass would listen."

I laughed. "Yeah, I think the last year made it clear to everyone that I won't."

A smile tugged at his own lips. "You want to stick around, then fine. The Spades can't say I didn't do my part to get you out, but now you've got bigger problems. You've got to play this a lot smarter."

"You honestly don't know who they are. The Spades."

He shook his head. "No one does. Not who or how many."

"But fear of them was enough for you to humiliate me in front of the planet."

Jaxson's face shuttered closed. He turned away.

"Why did you do it?" I pressed. "You admit you went too far, so why?"

"There is no excuse."

"I want one anyway. Tell me why."

The line of his jaw grew hard with tension. "Because... I was scared. I've heard the stories of the Spades, and the things they've done to people. The lives they've ruined. I didn't want me and Dad to be next." Sighing, Jaxson heaved himself up on his elbow and looked down at me. "I thought I was making the right choice. My family or you. But the truth is I was just being a coward."

I had never heard Jaxson talk like this before, and my head spun with everything he was telling me.

Jaxson placed a finger under my chin. Twin orbs of shining blue drew me in and drowned me. "I'm sorry, Valentina."

"They were wrong," I said so softly my lips barely moved. "You're not the stupid one."

A grin spread across his face. "That's what I keep telling people."

This time, it was me pushing him back down and settling into his arms.

"WON'T WE GET IN TROUBLE for this?" Jaxson plucked the chip from my hand and popped it into his mouth. "Hey."

We hadn't left my room all day, and by midnight our stomachs were letting us have it for the missed meals. Thankfully, I had plenty of junk stashed away.

"Get in trouble for what?" he asked.

"There are cameras all over this place so Gus knows you're here. Honestly, I've been waiting for him to bust the door down."

Part of me also might have been hoping he would bust the door down. This entire day didn't feel real. I couldn't comprehend being here with Jaxson, and a piece of me was still holding out that this was some evil trick. Jaxson hadn't pushed for us to do more than cuddle, but even if he did, I knew I couldn't let it happen. My heart wasn't in a place to trust him.

Jaxson paused the movie we were watching and shifted to face me. "Gus knows I'm a Knight. He won't be busting anything down."

I gaped at him. "So you're just allowed to come and go out of girls' rooms as you want? Is there no end to the things you guys are allowed to get away with?"

He laughed. "I still haven't managed to get Wheeldon off my ass so we can't get away with everything. For some reason that guy doesn't like me. What's that about? Everyone likes me."

I giggled. I could say a lot about Jaxson—and I have—but the guy did make me laugh. "He about busted a blood vessel the first time you called him 'homie.'"

He put up his hands. "Exactly. That's a mark of friendship and he almost lost his mind." He shook his head. "I just don't get that guy."

"You're such an idiot." I took a chip and shoved it into his mouth.

Jaxson chuckled between chewing. "No one around here likes the way I talk, but I see it as a plus that while my friends were taking *elocution* classes, I was running around the feet of the biggest names in music."

"I'd trade elocution classes for that in a hot second." I rested against my headboard. "Must have been amazing."

"It was." Jaxson's eyes slid off my face, becoming unfocused. "My mom wasn't about all this stuff. Money, cars, weekend trips to Europe. She grew up in a place a lot like your neighborhood, and met Papa Van Zandt when he was still searching dive bars for local talent."

"She was a singer?"

"No, a drummer. Dad said the first time he saw her, he had to come back the next time to listen to the band play because he spent the whole time out of it and just staring at her. I remember sitting on her lap while she played, but not much else. She died when I was five."

"I'm so sorry."

I took his hand in mind and he didn't waste the opportunity to lace our fingers together.

"She didn't want our family to be like the rest around here. Parents never around. Kids being raised by nannies and bank accounts. So when she passed, Dad kept his promise and brought me to work with him and... I loved it. Me and Dad are closer than most people are and the music I've gotten to listen to with him was incredible." The smile faded. "But I ruined that."

I lowered my eyes. "Jaxson, I'm—"

"No, don't apologize." The intensity in his voice made me meet his gaze. "I deserved what you did. We both know that."

"You did, but I only wanted to hurt you, not your dad or the label." I blew out a breath. "I love Levi Van Zandt. Not kidding. Love. If he asked, I'd be your stepmom in a heartbeat."

Jaxson's mouth fell open. "What the fuck, Moon?"

I clapped my hand over my mouth to hold in my laughter.

"Take it back."

"No."

"Do it."

"Never."

"That's it."

I squealed when Jaxson pounced. His fingers skittered all over my body as he tickled me into submission. We were both laughing so hard we couldn't breathe.

"Okay, okay!" I cried. "I take it back."

"Good." Jaxson hovered over me. His legs were splayed on either side as he straddled me. "Don't make me have to teach you this lesson again."

"You might," I teased. "I'm a stubborn ass, remember. I don't learn easy." I gripped his shoulders and shoved, pushing him down until our roles were reversed. "Can I ask you a question? It's something I've always wondered."

He nodded.

"How did you, Ezra, Maverick, and Ryder become friends? You guys aren't even kind of alike."

"What's that got to do with anything? You're nothing like Richards. She's as sweet as that honey her mom peddles, and you're as ruthless as it gets, and I mean that with mad respect."

I flicked him on the forehead.

"Ow. See what I mean?"

Rolling my eyes, I said, "Will you just answer the question?"

"Okay, okay." Jaxson fell back onto the pillow. His grin faded under a serious expression I rarely got to see. "We are different, but stuff like that doesn't really matter. Sometimes things happen—big things. And it binds people together so freaking tight that you have to be friends... because no one else will ever understand you like they do." He shook himself. "You probably don't get that—"

"I get it." I climbed off and lay down next to him. "I understand perfectly."

I HAD THE DREAM THAT night.

The awful routine of waking up gasping with my sheets soaked in sweat was not one I missed.

My fingers were clumsy as I reached for my hidden phone. I had Mom on the screen and my finger hovering over the call button when I stopped.

I hadn't had the dream in months, but after nearly being killed, I wasn't surprised it had come back.

Maybe part of me knew it would. That's why I sent Jaxson away.

It had been obvious that he wanted to stay, but I made him leave around three in the morning. I couldn't deny I had fun with him, nor could I deny that he had saved my life, but I was a long way off from sleepovers.

What are we now? I thought as I stripped my sheets. *Friends? Non-enemies? Two people who spend an afternoon eating chips and watching movies and then go back to avoiding each other?*

All I knew for sure is that my feelings toward the other Knights hadn't changed. Ryder and Maverick were still names begging to be taken off my list. Maybe being with Jaxson hadn't kept the dreams away, but planning revenge against him and the rest had.

"Next semester, I come back even harder."

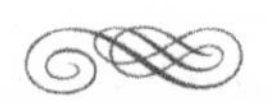

BY SOME MIRACLE, I got through my finals, and soon it was time to pack up and leave for break. Olivia honked her horn like a madwoman when I stepped through the gates.

"Whoo! There's my baby! Get over here!"

I rolled my eyes, but I wasn't fooling anyone. I dropped my bags and ran into her arms. Mom squeezed me until my stuffing came out. "I missed you, kid. This was a stupid idea letting you run off to some school hours away."

"Tell me about it." I looked past her and spotted Adam snoozing away in his car seat. "He's getting so big."

"Babies do that." She gave me a shake. "Except for mine. You'll be fun sized for the rest of your life."

Laughing, we rescued my things from the curb and beat it out of there. Sofia's driver was taking her straight to our place and I couldn't wait for three weeks of carols, Christmas cookies, and living room dance parties to begin.

"I've got a surprise for you," Olivia said when she paused in between telling me everything that had been going on. "A good one."

"Any hints?"

"Nope. Course not."

I pestered her through the whole drive anyway. Eventually, I gave up and turned to the window.

"Hey, wait. Why are we turning on Lincoln? Sofia is waiting for us at the apartment, Mom."

"No, she's not."

I gave her a crazy look. "Uhh, yes, she is. We can get Chinese delivered if you're hungry."

"I'm not hungry."

"Then why are we five minutes away from the Chinese place?"

"I can't help where the Chinese place is."

"Where are we going?"

"Where else would we be going?"

"Mom."

"Valentina."

I threw up my hands. "You're impossible."

She yukked it up, ignoring my stewing as she turned onto Devonshire Lane. I had only ever been to this part of town when Mom and I were on a Chinese food run. It was the only thing in this neighborhood we could afford.

Mom traveled between the rows of cute single-story houses painted in a variety of shocking pastels. I swallowed my annoyance as she parked in front of a light-blue house with flower boxes in the windows. "Mom, why are we here?"

"You wanted to go home so badly, and I took you. What more do you want?"

I froze as her words penetrated. "What?" I turned to face her and found her beaming from ear to ear. "You mean this is..."

"Our house, baby."

"B-but you— But you—" My head swung from her to the house, then to her, and then the house again. "But you didn't tell me!"

"That would have ruined the surprise, wouldn't it?" She patted my hand. "I'm not just working at the daycare now; I'm running it. I'm making enough to get us out of that puke-green hell and give my babies the home they deserve. What do you think?"

"Mom, it's so great." I felt myself getting choked up. I tried to stop it, but in seconds I was crying, then Mom was crying, then Adam woke up and he started crying. Sofia rolled up on a car full of blubbering messes.

The house was a perfect three-bedroom, two-bath paradise. Yes, paradise. Adam now had his own room and Mom had her own bathroom. My classmates had summer homes fifty times the size of this place, but this was everything we ever wanted.

The four of us didn't waste a second starting the best vacation of our lives. A few days before Christmas, Sofia and I were wrapping presents while Adam toddled around the living room. Mom was out food shopping so I finally had a chance to tell Sofia the secret I had been sitting on.

The scissors clattered to the floor, and I swiftly picked them up before Adam could set his sights on them. "You're a filthy liar."

"All true."

"You *did not* hook up with Jaxson Van Zandt and then wait this long to tell me!"

"Okay, hold up. I definitely did not hook up with him. We hung out and talked. That's it." I took a breath. "And it only happened because... someone tried again to kill me."

She paled. "Val, oh my gosh. Are you serious? How could you not tell me that?"

"I didn't want to scare you," I admitted. "I didn't see who it was, and I didn't know what more anyone could do besides assign me another bodyguard, and I won't take one who works for the school."

"Then what are you going to do?!" Sofia's voice was reaching new levels of high-pitched. The noise made Adam peer curiously at us. "You have to do something!"

"I will. The solution was obvious when I thought about it. I'm going to hire my own bodyguard."

"You— Wait. You can do that?"

"I'm going to Evergreen with it when we get back, but he'll have a hard time going against it after what the last one pulled."

"He better say yes, or I don't care what you say, I'm sticking to you like glue."

She pulled me in for a tight hug that only ended when Adam fell onto his backside and burst into wails.

I put the baby on my lap and gave him a bow to play with. He quieted instantly.

"Are you sure you're okay?" Sofia asked.

"I'm fine. I promise."

"Good." An expression came over her face that made my eyes widen. "Then I want every single detail about you and Jaxson, and don't think you can hold out on the dirty bits because Adam is here."

"There are no dirty bits!"

In spite of being grilled like a criminal, winter break was amazing. The only break in our weeks of laughing, celebrating, and having a good time was the call I had to put in to S, but I was careful to do that while I snuck off to the bathroom at Santa's village.

The usual sadness clung to me as we crested the hill to Evergreen Academy. Trading time with Adam and my mom for tyrannical headmasters and sneaking assassins was a hard sell.

I lifted my eyes and looked at Adam in the rearview mirror. Seeing him sitting there perfectly content staring out the window while he munched on his cookies, reminded me why I was doing this.

"I have people who depend on me."

"You keep that secret phone close by, kid. I'll be calling you at least three times a week and no buttoned-up fool is saying otherwise."

"Yes, Mom."

"And you nail your midterms this time so you can come home for spring break."

"I will."

Mom pulled up to the curb and killed the engine. "Alright. I love you. Be good, but not too good. You're allowed to break the stupid rules."

I was pretty sure no one else was getting that as a send-off.

"I love you, Mom." We hugged and kissed, then I leaned over the seat and did the same to Adam.

All too soon, I was standing on the edge of the curb waving goodbye as she drove away. It took me a minute to notice there was someone next to me doing the same.

"Such a shame," said Ryder. "It would have been so much better if you had been in that car driving away."

"Hello, Ryder. I would say that it was good to see you, but of course, it's not."

He tsked. "That comeback is kind of weak. I know you can do better than that."

"True. Give me a minute to wade through the indifference I have for your existence to see if I can care enough to try again. Oh, nope. Nothing," I finished without skipping a beat. I faced him with a smile. "But here is something I do care about. Did you ever have that chat with Dad?"

Ryder's expression didn't change. "You still on this? My dad's gone. Probably dead. If you think bringing it up is going to get to me, then you don't know me at all."

"Oh, we're talking about Benjamin Shea again?" I took a step closer to him. "Can I ask you something? Did you ask yourself why that guy ran around with all those women—cheating for the world to see?"

"Because the guy was a bastard." Ryder was so matter-of-fact you would have thought we were talking about the cafeteria lunch menu. "Next question."

"But that's not really why, is it?"

The granite was cracking—a frown marring his otherwise perfect feature. "What the fuck are you talking about?"

I didn't know that it would happen that day or like that. There was a time that I didn't think I'd be able to open my mouth and say these words at all, but standing before him in the haze of exhaust in front of the place that had morphed from my dream into my nightmare, the words fell from my lips as though it was always meant to happen like this.

"He didn't do it because he was a bastard, Ryder. He did it... because you are."

Chapter Seven

The granite crumbled.

Ryder's face went slack with shock, eyes wide as he stared at me like he had never seen me before. "What did you just say?"

"Come on, man. Don't look so shocked. I've been dropping hints for how long?" I flung every word at him like daggers. "Benjamin Shea is not your father."

"You— You—"

"No reason to be upset about it. The man was a bastard like you said. A truly awful shit human being," I spat. Anger roiled in my stomach—heaving and churning. It threatened the calm I was going for. "The way he acted in public was nothing compared to him in private. I know how he treated you and your mother."

"No, stop— Shut the fuck up!" he burst out. The mask was gone and Ryder couldn't reclaim it. His eyes bulged as starkly as the veins in his neck. "You're a fucking liar!"

I lifted my shoulders. "Fine. You don't have to believe me now, but I come with receipts. I'll prove it to you."

I picked up my bags and turned to go. I made it two steps before a hand seized my forearm. "Where do you—?"

"Miss Moon, is there a problem here?"

A man in a crisp, black suit peeled himself off the gates and strode up to us. Ryder's grip only got tighter.

"Who the hell are you?" he demanded.

The man didn't even look at him. "Miss Moon, my name is Sylvester Kane. I have been assigned as your personal security. Do you need me to step into this situation?"

"No, thank you, Mr. Kane." I gave Ryder a hard look. "He was just leaving."

Ryder looked at Kane like he was seriously considering his chances of taking him. In the end, he turned on me. "This isn't over."

"Course not," I said cheerily. "We have so much more to talk about."

He released me with a growl and stormed off.

"Okay," I said to Kane. "Let's get this over with."

Together, we joined the line leading through the gates and all the way to the academy courtyard. The line moved punishingly slow, but that's what happens when hundreds of students were forced to open their bags and have them searched.

It took an hour for us to finally reach Gus and his staff. They checked my bags, found nothing, and sent us on our way. We went straight to the headmaster's office.

"Hello. Is he in?"

The receptionist rang Evergreen up and then waved us on. He rose from his desk when we walked inside.

"What can I do for you, Miss Moon?"

I gestured at Kane. "You can allow my new bodyguard on campus so that he can protect me. That's all."

It was such a simple request, but Evergreen's eyebrows shot up his forehead. "Excuse me?"

"I can't trust anyone else after Noemi, but I'm clearly still not safe after the fire. Hiring my own security makes the most sense."

His frown deepened. "This is a closed campus. We don't allow anyone other than properly vetted staff to stay here. I understand your concerns, but the answer is no."

"I—"

Kane placed one massive hand on my shoulder. "Miss Moon, if you would allow me. We expected resistance, so my employer told me to give you this." Kane pulled a letter out of his coat pocket and held it out.

Evergreen made no move to take it. "I will not be swayed by Miss Moon's letter either."

"Miss Moon is not my employer."

The headmaster's self-assured expression twitched. Kane stared him down until he finally snatched the letter.

I watched Evergreen's face cycle through many emotions as he read the contents. By the time he looked up, he had settled on pissed. "Very well." He slammed the paper on the desk. "But you will meet with every term stated. Is that understood?"

Kane inclined his head.

"Leave my office."

I waited until we were in the hall to ask, "Any chance you'll tell me what the letter said?"

His silence answered well enough.

"Thought not." I waved him on. "Come on. My dorm is this way."

We weaved through the packed courtyard and escaped onto the grass. The noise faded as I led him into my building. "Where will you stay?" I asked as I pushed into my bedroom.

"The headmaster will provide rooms for me in the staff building. If you don't feel comfortable with that, my employer has offered to send my coworker Bea to remain here with you during the night."

"No, that's okay." I flung my bags on the bed. "You and I should get along fine, and I feel safe here now that Gus has replaced the windows. I guess we'll have to agree on times to meet since I can't text you."

He shook his head. "The no-phone rule does not apply to you. We need to be in constant contact. That was explained in the letter."

"Really?"

Kane proved it by pulling a cell phone out of his breast pocket. "This is yours. My number is programmed in."

"Wow. What else you packing in there?"

I was half-kidding, until Kane opened his coat and revealed his gun. My laughter dried up. "I will do everything in my power to protect you, Miss Moon."

"I don't doubt it," I croaked. "But, uh, I'm staying in for the rest of the day so you're good to go and get settled in."

He inclined his head and backed out. I waited until I heard the downstairs door close behind him before leaving my room. I slipped into one of the doors on the second floor, lifted the mattress, and scooped out the hammer, button cam, extra phone, disguise, and everything else I had been hoarding for my revenge.

I didn't know that the headmaster would search our rooms, but I wasn't taking a chance. The guy was still spitting over the leaked video. I took my things back to the room, sat on the bed next to my list. The first text I sent was to Alex.

Me: It's time. Pull the next trigger.

"I'M SO GLAD THIS STUPID ban is over," I overheard Natalie say. My new seat at the front was further from Maverick and Ezra, but closer to the Diamonds. "Dad tried to convince the headmaster that chess was academic and shouldn't be counted in with stupid things like football and drama, but he wouldn't budge. Now I'm behind a whole semester and the tournament is in a month."

Isabella looked over her compact mirror to give her friend a look. "You'll do well. You wouldn't be a Diamond if there was anyone who could compete with you." She cut eyes to Airi. "And now that you have a new violin, you can grab first chair."

"You've only told me that like a dozen times," Airi said with enough force to make me blink. "I get it already. I'll audition."

"Don't be like that, A," said Natalie. "We just can't stand to see you brought down by that slum trash. You don't want to lose your place as a Diamond."

Wow, who knew Natalie could get even more unpleasant.

"Hey, Moon."

Sighing, I turned to face them. "What do you want, Bard?"

"I saw you got a new bodyguard."

I twisted around to where Kane stood in the back—still and ever vigilant.

"I don't get it," she went on, "if you're so scared. Why are you still here?"

"You know, you care a lot about what I'm doing. It's starting to creep me out. Why don't you worry about yourself for a change?"

"You—!"

"I agree wholeheartedly," a stern voice cut in. Wheeldon peered at us over his laptop. "Concern yourself with reading and signing the new student guidelines, Miss Bard. Spend *less* time on Miss Moon."

A snicker fell from someone's lips. It was mine.

Natalie turned bright red, but didn't argue further. She ripped open the book and got to reading.

Finding these new handbooks on our desks the first day back wasn't a welcome surprise. In it were all the rule changes Evergreen made last semester, plus a few more thrown in. We had to sign them and agree to accept the consequences for having phones and speaking to the press. So much of this felt wrong, but if people like Madeline Richards didn't have lawyers strong enough to make him back down, then who could?

I signed the book and handed it back to Wheeldon at the end of class. A new semester meant new classes, and next up for me was Chemistry, according to my schedule. My head was bent over it when someone sidled up next to me.

"Hey, mama. Have a good break?"

I replied without lifting my head. "What are you doing, Jaxson? People are going to see you talking to me."

"And they'll think I'm hitting you up for sex as usual. You going to answer my question?"

"Yes, I had a good break."

"Nice. I did too." He sounded so relaxed, like we were two normal teenagers strolling through the halls. "I missed you though."

A flush crept up my neck. How could he say that so casually?

"Did you miss me?"

I roughly cleared my throat. "Normally I would have blown you off by now so you should go before it starts to look weird."

"One more thing. What did you do to my boy?"

"Have to be more specific. Everyone is your boy and your girl."

"Only one person is my girl."

I had no answer for that. I just kept my eyes on my schedule even though the words were blurring together.

"As for the boy I'm talking about, I mean Ryder. Dude's been acting like a zombie, and when I finally got a word out of him it was Valentina."

"I don't have a clue what that's about."

"Now, why don't I believe you?"

"We've covered this, Jaxson." I stopped dead making him stumble to a halt. We had arrived at the Chemistry classroom. "It's because you're not stupid."

He gave me the beginnings of a smile. "Don't wreck him too badly. He's not as bad as you think."

"You can tell me that when he's drowned, choked, and used your father against you."

Jaxson lost the smile completely. "Fair enough, but—"

"But what?"

"I thought you would have changed your mind about this revenge thing after..."

Jaxson didn't go on, but I was happy to do it for him. "After what happened between us?" I looked around to make sure no one was listening. "Just because we spent one day together and didn't kill each other, doesn't change what happened. I'm not going to stop." An awful thought occurred to me. "And if that's why you said all those things—"

"That was about you and me and no one else." He said that so firmly I wanted to believe him. "I'm not playing you, but I know why it's hard for you to believe that. How about I come over tonight and we talk?"

A part of me wanted that, but all of me knew what that talk would be about and I couldn't have it with him. "Tonight is not good. I'll be up to my neck in homework."

He nodded. "Fine. Tomorrow night. Until then, Moon."

"Wha— But I—"

Jaxson was already walking off.

Shaking my head, I entered the classroom and went for one of the desks.

"Don't get comfortable." I jumped. Turning around, I saw a man rise from behind the desk and squint at me through small, circular frames. "I will be assigning seats."

"Okay."

Not knowing what else to do, I still sat down and waited for the class to fill up. Professor Johnston made us get up as promised and named our lab partners and new seats. I ended up in the middle with Ciara.

"I need an A in this class," she announced the second she sat down. "So I don't have time to mess around."

"I don't do a lot of messing around. I leave that to you guys."

She frowned. "Look, we have to be lab partners, and no one expects us to mess up our grades for the marked, so you don't have to worry about me, but everyone knows you've been on some revenge kick since you got here, and if it's going to be a thing, I'm asking for a new partner."

"The only people who need to be worried are those who've given me a reason. Did you?"

She pressed her lips together and didn't speak another word to me for the rest of the lesson. After class ended, I swept out of the room for my next subject, my shadow trailing me only a few feet behind. Halfway to class, I realized something. No one was giving me nasty looks or hissing terrible things at me.

I thought after the break the effects of the video would have worn off and people would be ready to come after me again. Maybe they've decided they've had enough.

Or maybe it's the unfriendly-looking, gun-toting hulk of muscles staring everyone down like he's ready to pop their heads like a grape. Cowards like an easy target.

That sounded a lot more likely, but whatever the reason, I wasn't worrying about it. I needed to focus on bigger fish. If Alex had done what they said, and they always did, then Maverick was in for a surprise.

I STOPPED NEXT TO MY locker and turned to Kane. "You don't need to come with me to lunch."

"I'm to be with you at all times."

"I have my phone, and I'll be in a room full of witnesses. I'll be okay. Please go."

He didn't budge.

"Okay," I drew out. "Then how about this? Whatever you see me do, will you keep it to yourself?"

"I am bound by nondisclosure agreements. They extend to you."

This I didn't know. "That's perfect. In that case, you can come to lunch with me."

Kane trailed me to the cafeteria and up to the lunch line. There was usually a hush that fell onto the room when I walked in, but this time I didn't think it was me. The large man joined me at my table and made unsettling eye contact with everyone who looked my way. He was no Noemi, but that might have been what I liked about him.

The Knights strode into the room and headed for the dais. As they sat, I stood.

"Let's go."

Kane got to his feet and followed me through the double doors. He was my silent shadow as I made one stop at my locker for my bookbag, and then continued on my way.

The door to the Knights' room was closed, and by a test of the handle, locked. My eyes swept the hallway while I dug around in my backpack. The academy still hadn't gotten around to putting cameras in the hallway.

More fool them.

I hefted the hammer over my head...

...and brought it down on the lock with all my strength.

The wood splintered as the metal bent. Another hit and the spiderweb of cracks grew. I hit it again and the handle went flying off, skidding across the floor.

I glanced at an expressionless Kane. "Wait out here."

"I'd like to sweep the room first."

I didn't fight him. Shoving my way inside, I leaned against the ruined door while Kane checked the few nooks and crannies for attackers. When he was done, I stepped aside and he closed the door behind him without a word.

The hammer was held tightly between my fist as I descended on the coffee table. Maverick had been a tough one to plan for. He kept to himself. His only close friends were the Knights. He dreamed of taking over his dad's company, but so did most of the people around here, and he didn't have any precious items like a violin from his grandfather. The only thing I knew he really cared about was being able to code and build things, and short of breaking his fingers, there was no way for me to take that away.

The massive virus I had Alex infect his systems with was mostly fair play. He attacked me, so I came for him. But I came in their personal space for another reason...

I smashed the hammer on a tiny little robot thing and watched it burst apart into a dozen soaring pieces. Every single sleek, techy, handmade piece of hardware was reduced to nothing in the face of my wrath. I couldn't break his fingers, but I could destroy the things those fingers created like he had destroyed my hard work.

There was a beautiful symmetry in what I was doing. I only wished I could see his face when he saw how I had completed our story and brought things full circle.

MAVERICK STUMBLED INTO homeroom the next morning white as a sheet. The other Knights came in behind him all shooting me different looks. Jaxson looked resigned. Ezra like he was barely restraining himself, and Ryder...

I wanted to look away from those eyes but held them with difficulty. Still a feeling like being shoved in a freezing shower overcame me. Ryder tended toward perfection like Ezra did. His uniform was always neat and his hair styled.

Not today. His raven locks were swept up in a wild fashion that made him look like he had just gotten out of bed, and his shirt was half buttoned and half out of his pants.

I sharply tore my attention away from Ryder when two hands smacked onto my desk. Maverick towered over me, blocking the artificial lights and casting a shadow almost as long as the one on his face. "Everything destroyed."

"Mr. Beaumont," Wheeldon spoke up. "Have a seat."

I heard the heavy, rapidly approaching footsteps of Kane and wondered what he was going to do.

"You're a man of few words, Maverick, but you're going to have to give me more information than that."

Maverick's hand shot off the desk. I stiffened, but it wasn't me that hand was after. Maverick reached into his pocket and yanked something out. "You destroyed everything."

I held my breath as he dropped a green piece of twisted metal on my desk.

"This one was for you."

"Mr. Beaumont." Kane appeared at my side. "You were told to go to your seat."

I stared at the green piece long after he left. I didn't even remember what it had been a part of.

"This one was for you."

Why would he have made me anything? What am I supposed to do with that?

Unease twisted my stomach into knots as my hand closed over the metal. How had he done that? I had finished our story. Used my revenge to close the door on the boy I had my first crush on, and with one sentence and some stupid piece of broken toy, he cracked it back open.

I SOUGHT SOFIA OUT in the lunchroom that afternoon. She caught my eye and I tapped the tip of my milk carton three times. She responded by taking her hair out of its ponytail and redoing it. It was sad that we were reduced to hand signals and codes, but as long as I got to hang out with my best friend, it was worth it.

I went back to my room after dinner that night and promised I was staying in. I watched Kane disappear from my bedroom window while I shoved on my shoes. I was out the door and running across the courtyard five minutes later.

The main building was locked this time of night so I skirted around it to the quad. It wasn't late so there were still some people around, sitting on the benches and enjoying the masterpiece of colors from the setting sun. I heard running behind me, but I didn't pay it any mind until a hand on my arm pulled me back.

"Hey!"

"Where are you going?" The chilled voice that slid into my ear was unmistakable. "And where is your bodyguard?"

Ryder stepped into my line of sight, blocking my path. I pressed my lips together while his silver eyes swept me up and down.

"It's good that we're finally alone. We have a lot to talk about."

"We have nothing to talk about. What more do I need to say?"

"You need to tell me when you fell and got brain damage, because that's the only explanation for the shit you were spouting outside the gates."

"It's not shit." I took a step back and Ryder moved with me, not allowing a hair's width of distance between us. "Everything I said was true."

"Benjamin Shea is my father."

"He's not." I tried again to move away. Ryder's hand flashed out and encircled my wrist. Not hard enough to hurt, but to get his point across. He wasn't letting me go anywhere.

"You don't know what you're talking about."

I cocked my head. "I don't know what I'm talking about? I know he found out you weren't his. I know he couldn't stand that. The parade of lovers through the media was on purpose—to get back at your mother for cheating on him... and to get an heir that wasn't another man's."

"No." The word fell from Ryder's lips so easily. He didn't look mad. No, at that moment the mask was firmly in place. He was my cold marble statue once again, and he didn't believe a word I was saying.

"You didn't wonder why?" I pressed. "Why would the great Benjamin Shea, respected member in the industry, sink so low that the media would trash him and his own board would be pushed to the brink of outing him? He didn't care about any of that, Ryder. He just wanted to—in his eyes—set things right."

"You're a liar."

"Find his will, Ryder, and you'll see for yourself. It's set up for someone else to take your place."

"No, it's not."

I curled my fists. I could take anger, rage, yelling, and violence, but this cold denial was infuriating.

"You don't have to believe me now," I forced out, "but I can prove it."

He raised a brow. "Then do it, Moon. Let's see this proof."

"I don't have it on me."

"You don't have it at all. It doesn't exist."

I closed the scant amount of distance between us. Rising up, my lips brushed against his as I whispered, "Your denial will only make it sweeter when I prove you wrong. I'm telling you the truth, Ryder. Deep down, you know it's true."

"Nothing you say is true," he replied, "and the only thing that will be sweet is the look on your face when I make you pay for this."

"We'll see." I tugged on my arm and he let go without a fight. I sidestepped him and kept going like he never got in my way. Sofia was waiting in our spot like arranged. She jumped off the couch when she saw me.

"Val, finally! Is everything okay?" She grabbed my hand and pulled me down next to her. "I know you got to Maverick, but you should know Evergreen isn't pleased about the Knights' room being broken into."

"Then he should get cameras for those hallways like a normal school, but then how would the Spades sneak around?"

"If only we could put up cameras and find them." She blew out a breath. "I don't know what else we can do. We've looked at every picture I could find of the party, and I've asked around. No one remembers who wore what."

"I know. I've accepted at this point that the only person who can tell me what I need to know is Ryder."

She blew out a breath. "But he'll never do that."

"He might... once I've broken him so badly there's no part strong enough to say no."

Sofia blinked. "Val?"

"It's time, Sofia. I said what was between us couldn't be settled by anyone else. It had to be me and after all this, it's finally time."

"Are you sure about this?"

I nodded.

"When will you do it?"

"I'll know when."

We stayed on the roof for a bit longer but the mood had shifted. Soon I left and hurried across the lawn to the safety a dozen security cameras could bring. When I pulled the covers to my chin that night, I knew what was coming.

WIDE, TERRIFIED EYES disappeared in the gush of blood. It flowed down the knife—hot and thick and seeking my fingers.

I couldn't think for the awful, piercing screams that filled the air. They covered the even more horrible sound of frenzied gasping.

I didn't understand what was going on? The screaming was so loud. It scrambled my already sluggish thoughts.

Why wouldn't they stop? Why wouldn't they—

Oh, wait...

I put my hand to my raw, aching throat and smeared it with blood.

The person screaming was me.

EVERYONE WAS EXCITED for the first day of dance practice since the headmaster's rampage, but my mind was on other things. My eyes kept straying to my backpack and what lay within.

"Valentina, are you with us?"

I shook myself. "Sorry, Yvette. I'm listening."

She nodded. "Okay, pay attention, everyone." We were gathered on the mat, forming a semicircle around her. "We missed the regionals' qualifying competition last semester, so unfortunately, there is no way we can make it to nationals."

A string of curses fell from a few mouths and Yvette didn't comment on it. She was as mad as we were about club activities being canceled.

"We can't change that, but we can work hard to be ten times as good when our chance comes around again."

Eric raised his hand. "What are we supposed to do this semester if we're not competing?"

"There is still the opportunity for some of you to enter individual competitions. There is one in particular that I have my eye on for Valentina."

I perked up. "Really? Me? That would be—"

"What competition?" Isabella broke from the group and planted herself in front of Yvette.

"It's hip-hop, but they only accept solo dancers." Yvette found me over her shoulder. "Are you interested?"

"Definitely."

Isabella moved back in the way. "I am too. That's not fair. You should allow us all the chance to compete."

"Isabella, we should discuss this another time."

"But I've been training," she insisted. "My ballet instructor told Mother that hip-hop teaches dancers creativity and body expression, and after my audition for the part of Clara was named 'inspired and inventive,' she hired Vibes Taranto to be my personal teacher."

Shocked gasps went through the group. My mouth fell open and Isabella turned just in time to catch it before I snapped it shut. She smirked. "I can do the competition, Yvette."

Yvette was still spinning about Vibes. "You've been training with Taranto? Incredible, Isabella."

Incredible was right. The guy was a legend. A singer-songwriter-dancer and famous member of a hip-hop group that was named after him. A few years ago, he retired and opened his own studio for the rich and famous.

"Well, if you feel you're ready, you're welcome to enter the competition with Valentina."

Her triumph was clear on her face. Was I supposed to feel honored that she was working this hard to top me? All I knew for sure was that she could hire as many instructors as she wanted; I was not losing this competition.

I made it through the rest of practice and walked with Kane back to my dorm. I slowed down when I saw the lone figure leaning against my door.

Kane put an arm out in front of me. "Are you expecting him?"

"Yes, I am." I pushed his arm down. "Can you give us some privacy?"

"I will not listen, but I will keep you in sight."

That would have to do. Sighing, I stepped up to Jaxson. "You shouldn't have come," I started, skipping over the hello.

"I told you I was coming."

He peeled himself off the door and stepped to the side. "Let's go inside. It'll be like last time."

I wanted that. Damn, it hurt me how much I wanted that. But I couldn't do it.

"Last time shouldn't have happened. I'm so thankful you saved me, but I was scared and not thinking straight. There is nowhere for you and me to go, Jaxson."

His grin faded. I said I never saw serious Jaxson, but he was becoming all too familiar to me.

"Why do we have to go somewhere? Why can't this just be what it is?"

"It's not that simple. How can it be after everything we have done to each other?"

"I've forgiven you."

"But I haven't forgiven *you*." The words struck him nearly as hard as it struck me. Jaxson staggered back as the band wrapped around my lungs. "You don't know what that day in the auditorium did to me, Jaxson. You broke me. I cracked under Ryder, Maverick, and Ezra, but it was you who delivered the killing blow. You don't get to just say a few sweet words to make it all go away."

"And what will make it go away?" Bright spots of color stained Jaxson's cheeks. So many emotions battled for dominance in his expression that I couldn't place one. "Will wrecking Maverick's computers do it? Turning Ezra's mom against him? Breaking a violin? Is that what's going to put you back together?"

"It can't make things worse."

"I wouldn't be too sure about that, mama."

I swallowed, not trusting myself to say anymore.

Shaking his head, Jaxson came closer and did something I wasn't ready for. He placed a light kiss on my forehead. "I don't have the right to push after what I did. If you don't want this, I'll go."

A thousand replies sprang to my lips but I didn't voice any of them as Jaxson kissed me once more. I watched him go until Kane prompted me to go inside. I went in without comment. I had things to do. Names to cross off a list. I couldn't think about Jaxson Van Zandt and something that never was.

Chapter Eight

I stared at the dais. My class blurred around the edges of my vision as I focused solely on Ryder.

He got closer and closer until I realized I was moving. My feet were carrying me to him. In my hand, I held one single sheet of paper. Silence descended on the room as I stepped onto the dais. The Knights stopped talking mid-stream and four pairs of eyes looked at me.

It was good I was doing it this way. For once, I controlled the situation. No Ryder tracking me down and demanding I meet his terms. I placed the paper in front of him with no flourish—almost like setting down a menu.

"You wanted proof," I announced. "Here it is."

"What?" He didn't look down.

"Everything I said was true, Ryder. See for yourself."

I was backing away when he finally glanced at the paper. Off the dais and past the lunch line when his eyes widened and he snatched it up. He began shouting when I reached the doorway, and the last thing I saw before it swung shut was him fighting to get out of Jaxson and Maverick's hold.

THE NEXT FEW DAYS, Kane stuck to me like glue. The man was no dummy; he saw in Ryder's eyes the same thing I did. I had thought that Ryder was beginning to crack, but giving him that paternity test took away all doubt. The icy mask had been pulverized, and all that remained was the real him.

Ryder tried more than once to get to me. Kane stopped him in the halls and in class, but that didn't prevent him from banging on my door in the middle of the night, shouting for me to come out. The guy was unraveling like a frayed shoelace, and every day, he got more rumpled, sleep-deprived... and angry.

Saturday saw me in my room with no plans to come out. I was getting comfortable with my laptop when I heard another knock from downstairs. That it wasn't wild pounding made me get up and see who it was.

I blinked through the window. Sofia waved.

"What are you doing here?" I asked when I threw open the door.

"Relax. I made sure no one saw me." She came inside and we went up to my room. "I wanted to see how you were doing. The last few days have been insane."

"I know." I flopped on my bed. "Ryder's taking it about as well as I thought he would."

"He's not here you know." The mattress dipped as she lay down next to me. "He got permission to go off campus and left this morning."

"I hope he's gone all weekend. I'd like one night without his banging."

"Gus should get him to stop that."

"I don't think he'll do anything unless the guy breaks in. I'm surprised he hasn't tried that."

"Val, I think he's losing it. I know it must be hard finding out your father isn't who you think he is, but I didn't think he'd react like this."

My eyes traced the curves and beams of the four-poster bed. "I did. I knew this would reach him like nothing else would."

She placed her hand on mine. "At least you've gotten back at the Knights. You can cross Ryder off your list now and move on."

I wish that were true.

Sofia pulled me up and queued the movie. I appreciated that we didn't have to talk more because I didn't know what to say. How did I tell her that I didn't feel any better? How did I admit that Jaxson had been right? I thought that getting revenge would fix me, but if striking back at Ryder hadn't done it, then how could I believe that Natalie or Isabella would?

I'll always feel this way. I rested my hand on my chest. *Like I can't breathe.*

THAT NIGHT I WENT TO the sports complex. I didn't call Kane. I didn't want him to know about my secret spot. I liked that it was a place that was just mine where no one could reach me.

I sucked in a deep lungful of air as I stepped out onto the roof. The couch beckoned me and I spread myself on its cushions to look up at the stars.

It's crazy how beautiful it is up here. Don't know how Sofia stumbled on this but I have no clue where I'd be without it.

I don't know how long I lay there, but it was long enough that I snapped out of my doze when I heard the creak of the door.

"Oh, hey, Sofia." I rubbed at my eyes. "I thought you said you had homework."

"How did you know?"

I stilled, my hands pressed to my eyes as that voice slipped into my mind and wiped it blank with panic.

"Ryder?" I lowered my hands, but my sight only confirmed what I didn't want to be true. *How did he find me?*

"Jaxson wasn't good at it so I had Ezra follow you."

I hadn't realized I had asked the question out loud. My lips were so numb I didn't feel them move.

"He told me you slipped in somewhere behind the gym... alone." The door closed behind him with a click that reverberated in my soul. "I came back as quickly as I could."

"Why?"

Ryder's raven hair hung in clumps around his face and covered his eyes. He took a step and I swung my feet down and stood.

"How did you know?" Ryder lifted his hand and I saw what he had been hiding behind his back. The paternity test stood stark between us. The thing that had started it all. "Tell me."

He took another step causing me to back up. This wasn't good. Ryder's voice was too calm. His movements too controlled. I didn't know who this was.

"Ryder, I get you're upset, but—"

"You knew about the will too." He came closer. One, two, three steps, and me doing the same. "You knew it said that if a second heir stepped forward, they were entitled to everything. The homes, the business, the money, and not a cent left for me and Mom.

"You knew." Ryder moved into the light. It beat back the shadows on his face until I could see his eyes clearly. An unseen hand clamped my throat and squeezed. Dread surged through my veins. I always had the feeling that Ryder wanted to hurt me. In that moment, I knew that he did... I knew that he would. "Tell me how you knew."

"I'm not telling you." I was proud of my voice for not shaking. "I'm especially not telling you on this roof while you're having some kind of breakdown." I steeled myself. "I'm leaving, Ryder. Move out of the way."

I took a step—just one—and his eyes flashed. I knew what he was going to do before he moved.

"Ryder!"

I tried to run but there was nowhere for me to go. Ryder was on me in seconds, grabbing my arms.

"Get off!" I yanked out of his grasp and stumbled against the ledge. I fell down hard, and the momentum pushed me over. I screamed as gravity pulled at me until it was choked off by a gasp. Ryder's fist closed on my collar.

"P-pull me up! Pull me up!"

My feet scrabbled for purchase. The tips of my shoes kicked against the roof, but couldn't get footing. I clawed at Ryder, reaching for him.

"Help me!"

He didn't move. All he had to do was open his hand and I would be gone. I wondered if he was thinking that as I looked into his eyes... and found nothing.

No rage. No mercy. No fear. No sadness.

The wind was blowing against my back, tugging and pushing me back over the side, but its strength wouldn't be enough to carry me if he let go.

I twisted my neck and peered down at the unforgiving drop. This was it. It would all end here.

I guess I knew when I started this that it could only end one way. I wish I could say I would have done things differently, but the truth is, I wouldn't have changed a thing.

I swore they would all know my pain... and after this, I won't know pain at all.

Turning back, I let my eyes flutter shut and let go.

"He raped me."

The hand on my collar twitched—only the slightest movement—but it spurred me on.

"Benjamin Shea raped me... and not once."

"W-what?"

I didn't open my eyes. I couldn't if I was going to do this. "He was having an affair with my mother. He'd come by the apartment at night to see her and after she f-f-fell asleep, he would c-come into my r-room.

"He found out you weren't his son and wanted a true heir. My mom was another in a long line of women he chose to make that happen, but after months she still wasn't pregnant. None of them were." Tears fell hot and fast down my cheeks. "He thought the problem was he was sleeping with old hags when what he really needed was fresh p-pussy. That's what he said to me the first time he did it."

"V-Val... no."

"Yes!" I screeched. "*He* is how I knew. He told me e-e-everything."

I was gasping worse than ever. There was no air. All of it had been sucked from the night leaving me to die in a cold, empty vacuum. The grip on my throat squeezed and squeezed forcing the words back down. There was only one more thing I needed to say.

"He told me... about the will," I rasped. "He said... everything would go to his... biological son." Chest heaving, I peeled my eyes open and met those silver-grays. "It was the last thing he s-said to me... before I killed him."

His eyes widened—fathomless orbs growing white around the edges, and then I was falling.

Ryder disappeared as the stars filled my vision. At least their beauty would be the last thing I saw.

Chapter Nine

"Valentina!"

I went swinging over the side. My legs flew up—

—and were caught by two strong arms.

The world blurred as I smacked into the side of the building. I hung upside down, screams ripping from my throat as I flailed desperately.

"Ryder, help! Help!"

A hard tug and I flew over the ledge. Ryder and I collapsed in a heap on the roof, both breathing so hard I could hear it over the roaring in my ears.

The trouble breathing was part my own panic, but it could have also been due to Ryder. He clung to me so tightly, crushing me to his chest, I felt his pounding heart against my rib cage.

"Are you okay? Are you okay?" I was not the only one panicking. "Fuck! Tell me you're okay?"

"I'm... okay."

Ryder put his hand on the back of my head. I panted against his neck as he pulled me closer. "I'm s-sorry. Fuck, I'm so sorry, Val."

I froze. He was what?

I might have moved. Pulled away. Something. But overcooked noodles would have done a better job holding me up than my limbs would. I don't know how long we lay there in the dark, but my breathing slowed by the time Ryder roused himself.

Ryder pushed himself up and dragged us over to the couch. He propped me against it, then he fell back on my other side.

"You almost killed me," I stated. There was no heat or venom in the words. I said them as plainly as someone would say they had put butter on their toast.

"You killed my father." His tone matched mine.

"I killed the man you thought was your father."

"How?"

I kept my gaze fixed ahead. "You really want to know?"

"Yes."

My brain couldn't offer up a reason to lie to him, so I told him. "It wasn't until after that I found out he was drugging my mom to keep her from stopping him. That night, he came over, and they had dinner. He poured her a glass of wine and looked at me while I did the dishes. I knew what he was going to do—knew it as my hand reached for the knife."

I took a shuddering breath and Ryder didn't try to fill the silence. After a minute, I kept going. "I only wanted to scare him—make him leave me alone. I never thought I would use it." The words were coming easier. "That night Mom was ripped out of a drugged sleep by stomach cramps. She heard what was going on and ran into my room. Mom pulled him off of me, but she was sick and he was too strong. He hit her. They struggled... and my lamp fell over and shattered. He held her down and reached for one of the shards, and before I knew it the knife was in my hand—"

"That's enough. You don't have to say anymore."

That wasn't what stopped me. What made the words die in my throat was the hand that reached across my lap and took mine.

"You don't have to say anymore," he repeated.

Looking down at our hands, I sighed. "Yes, I do. I opened this door. I can't close it again." I said that but it was a while before I continued. "Mom took me out of there after it happened. She bathed me and cleaned me up all the while saying 'Everything is going to be okay. Mommy is going to make it okay. I promise.'

"Then she put me in her bed. When I woke the next morning, the body was gone... and your mother was there."

Ryder jerked. The act went through our hands and shook me. "My mom?"

"Yes, your mom."

"But that's not—"

"I wouldn't start lying to you now," I interrupted, and he fell silent. "She was sitting at the kitchen table with my mother like that was where she was meant to be. I don't know what they talked about or what my mother said to get her there, but she told me she had taken care of the situation. Benjamin was gone, and she would see that I had everything I needed to have a normal life. A few weeks later, I found out I was pregnant."

I looked at him now. The fairy lights cast their glow on his sickly pale skin. Sick was the right word to use. Ryder clutched his stomach with the other hand like he was going to throw up. "P-pregnant?"

"With Adam," I finished. "Your mother came to me when she found out. She promised she would help me, she only wanted one thing."

He nodded—a slow, jerky movement. "The will."

"Growing in my belly was the baby that could destroy your entire lives. She said she would give me whatever I wanted if I never brought Adam forward as his son, which is something I would have agreed to for nothing at all." My lips twisted. "I won't have the world seeing him as Adam Shea—that bastard's son. He is Adam Moon and that is who he will always be.

"I told your mom as much, but she insisted. She said Benjamin had done so much evil, and that the best revenge was living happily in his wake. Only Adam and I would suffer as a teenage mom living in the projects. I still said no, but then she came back with that paternity test."

"My mom... gave you the test?"

"She did. Caroline told me this wasn't a bribe, it was trust. We were trusting each other to do what was best for our sons, and she was showing it by giving me the one thing that could ruin her. So she opened up a bank account and helped me get what I really wanted: entrance into this school. Kids from Wakefield go nowhere, but someone who graduates from here has their pick."

I looked hard at him as I said, "That's why I'll never leave. It was blood, and pain, and agony that brought me here, but it's Adam that makes me stay. I'm going to give him the best life that I can."

"Okay." He still wasn't looking at me. I tried to pick out any sort of emotion on his face, but it was blank. What he was thinking, I couldn't possibly begin to guess.

"Don't you want to say more than that?" I glanced down at our hands. "Ryder, I need you to say something."

He opened his mouth, and I braced myself for what was coming next.

"My fa— Benjamin was a bastard anyway."

Ryder released my hand. I said nothing as he got to his feet and walked away, closing the door softly behind him.

I'M NOT SURE WHAT I expected to happen after what Ryder and I went through on the roof, but whatever those hopes were, they were dashed. Weeks went by without him speaking to me, looking at me, breathing in my direction. I didn't know how to feel about it except there was no edge to it. It didn't seem like he was ignoring me, he simply didn't know what to do any more than I did.

That was fine at first, I was still reeling at having shared those things with him, but as one week became two, and then two became three, I accepted that I needed more than that. "My father was a bastard anyway," was something I wholeheartedly agreed with, but I had to know how he felt. We had to talk.

My revenge plan stalled as that thought consumed me. How was I going to get him to talk to me? I wish it was as simple as walking up to him, but no one got Ryder to do anything he didn't want to do. I couldn't make him be honest with me if he was determined this wall of silence remain.

"There's only one week left."

I tore myself out of my thoughts. "What?"

Sofia grabbed my pillow and whacked me over the head. Getting away with visiting me the first time had made her bold, and she had taken to sneaking over after curfew. I told her not to risk it, but she'd ignore me and show up anyway.

"You've been so out of it, Val. What's up?"

I shrugged. "I don't know. I guess I thought striking back against the Knights would feel better than this."

"Does that mean you want to forget about Isabella and Natalie?"

"No, I— Ugh! I don't know." I smashed my face into the pillow, and soon felt Sofia's hand on the back of my head.

"I think rule number five can extend to this. Knowing when you've gone too far can also be knowing when you've had enough. Isabella and Natalie are sad little bullies obsessed with attention and they *never* deserved yours. Let them live their pathetic lives while we focus on who is really important—the Spades."

I lifted my head. "Who we will never find unless I can get Ryder to tell me what he knows. That's just more reason why I need to talk to him."

"I wish you could."

"You know what... no." I pushed myself up. "We can't do this anymore. My life has been turned upside down and I've almost been killed twice. I'm going to make him talk to me."

"How are you going to do that?"

I clambered off the bed. "I have no idea."

"At least you've thought it through."

Her sarcasm followed me into the closet but I waved it away. I grabbed the first thing I saw and pulled it on. I was going. I was doing this.

"Do you want me to come with you?" she asked while I bent under the bed.

"No, I have to do this myself."

I found my shoes, jammed them on my feet, and was out the door. I sped across campus, determination lighting a fire under me.

He will talk to me. I'm not taking no for an answer. He will.

I marched up to the sophomore dorms and burst through the doors.

He will talk to me.

The elevator dinged on the second floor... and that's when reality hit me smack in the face. What the hell was I doing? Not only did I have no clue *how* I was going to get him to talk to me, I also didn't know which room was his.

I looked between 202 and 208 and chose at random. The door flew open a few minutes after my knock and Jaxson stood before me in nothing but a pair of boxers.

"Valentina?" He looked as surprised to see me as I was to see him in his underwear.

You've seen more than that. My cheeks heated up.

"What are you doing here?" He gestured over his shoulder. "Did you want to come in?"

"No, I'm looking for Ryder. Which room is his?"

He blinked. "Ryder? Ryder Eugene Shea? That Ryder?"

"His middle name isn't Eugene."

"Nah, but it pisses him off when I tell people it is."

I bit back a smile. How was he still making me laugh—even at a time like this?

Jaxson pointed down the hall. "He's 208."

"Thanks." I turned to go.

"Will you hit me up after? I wouldn't mind another Saturday curled up in bed with you."

I stopped. "Jaxson, we talked about this."

"I can hold out hope that you've changed your mind."

"Not yet." I picked up my feet and kept going.

"Yet?" he called after me. "That means I have a chance."

Shaking my head, I hid another smile as I knocked on the right door. This wasn't the time. *I can't think about my feelings for anyone else until I speak to—*

"Finally, Ezra." A rush of steam came through the door as Ryder stepped into the entrance. A thick fluffy towel covered his head and face, matching perfectly with the one tied low on his waist. "I told you to bring my shaving cream back an hour ago."

—Ryder.

"I don't have shaving cream." Ryder ripped the towel off his head. "But I hope I can still come in."

He gaped at me—face showing surprise like I had seen only once before. I stepped closer. "Can I come in?" I repeated.

"Uh... yeah." He quickly moved out of the way. "Go ahead."

I walked in, not stopping until I was in the middle of the room. Ryder's room looked the same as my old one except where I had pictures of Adam and Mom, Ryder had photos of him and the Knights. My feet carried me to a frame on his nightstand. Ezra, Maverick, Jaxson, and Ryder smiled back at me. Their young faces fresh and adorable as they posed with their arms around each other, all in their junior prep school uniform.

"One second."

I turned as Ryder disappeared into his bathroom. *I'm really doing this. This is happening.*

I sat down in his desk chair and attempted to steady my nerves. I had told this guy I had been sexually assaulted, committed murder, and became a mother at fourteen. He knew every one of my deepest secrets, but deep down, I felt like I knew nothing about him.

The bathroom door opened again and Ryder walked out in a white tee and gray sweatpants. Water dripped from his hair onto the towel slung around his shoulders and the dark scruff on his chin told of why he needed the shaving cream.

Ryder sat on the edge of his bed, allowing an entire floor rug to separate us. "Is something wrong?"

My hands fisted on the hem of my dress. "Of course, there's something wrong. We need to talk, Ryder. I've been waiting weeks for you to come to me, but I can't wait any longer."

He frowned. "For me to come to you? But, Val, I— I didn't think you'd want that."

"What do you mean?"

"For me of all people to make you talk about what you went through. You shouldn't have to relive that with me. Not after the things I've done to you."

"Oh." Of all the reasons I thought of for why Ryder wasn't speaking to me, being considerate of my feelings hadn't cracked the top twenty. "I get that," I began, "but we need to talk about it. I've been going crazy wondering what you're going to do or say—"

Ryder's frown deepened. "Say? I would never tell anyone what you told me."

I swallowed. "But I... killed the man who raised you."

"It was self-defense." Ryder's silver eyes weren't blank now. They shone with an emotion I had never seen before. "And my mother helped cover it up so telling the truth of what happened hurts both of us." He got to his feet. "If you came here because you were worried I wouldn't keep your secret, you don't have to be."

"Ryder, it's not just that." Suddenly, I was on my feet too. "You know what almost happened on that roof. Things have always been"—I waved my hands—"insane between us! We do too much; we go too far, and I have never understood why because I don't know how you feel! So for once, tell me!" I crossed that stupid rug and didn't stop until I was in front of him, inhaling his piney scent. "Tell me how you feel about this. Tell me where we go from here."

Ryder looked down on me, his lips unmoving. I waited but he didn't speak. Finally, I turned away. "Goodbye, Ryder."

"I knew about the affair."

I froze. "What?"

"Your mom and Benjamin. I knew."

"How?"

Ryder ripped the towel off his neck and threw it on the chair I just vacated. "I walked in on them in his office. I was twelve. She didn't see me, but he did." He tossed his head. "I went at him that night, expecting him to show some shred of guilt, but he told me to shut up and pushed me away. He said..."

Ryder's arms bulged as his hands curled into fists.

I don't know what made me do it, but I reached for him. Taking his hand, I pulled us both down onto the bed.

"What did he say?"

"He said that he'd have a new kid and a new wife soon, so why should he give a fuck about us?"

My jaw dropped. "He said that to you?"

"He did and I thought... that wife and kid was you and Olivia."

"Oh my gosh." I lowered my head as it began to make sense. "That's why you hated me."

"My mother was too depressed to leave her bedroom while another woman screwed her husband down the hall, and her kid ran around her house. Yes, I hated you. I hated your mother, but most of all, I hated him. But of all those people, the only one I could hurt was you."

I felt sick to my stomach. "I didn't know about them until he started coming to the apartment."

"I understand that now."

"No one wanted him out of our lives more than me," I cried. "If he had married my mother, I would have killed myself! I couldn't—"

"Valentina. I'm sorry."

Those quiet words silenced me faster than a shout ever could.

"I'm sorry," he repeated. There was no mask. Ryder's grief was there for me to see. "If I had known... I never would have been so awful to you, and that's still no excuse. I'm a piece of shit and sorry will never begin to cover it."

"But you see that now?"

"Of course, I do. Val, he r— He ra—" Letting out a shout, Ryder launched himself off the bed and began to pace. "He hurt you. A grown man doing those things to you— You had been through enough." His hand flashed out and punched the desk. "I hate that I made it worse."

"Ryder..."

"Was it him?" Ryder raised his head, letting me see the fire in his eyes. "Did he give you chlamydia?"

It took me a while, but I nodded.

"Motherfucker!"

Another punch made me jump.

I kept my voice low. "Ryder, you seem angry."

"Of course I'm angry!"

"No... you seem angry *for me*."

He rocked back. His distress was overcoming him. Tossing his head, Ryder gripped the back of his chair until his knuckles turned white. "I'm angry for you. People shouldn't do things like this, Val. Kids. Just kids! Why do they do it?!"

The chair shot away under his assault and Ryder fell against the desk.

"Ryder?" Concern laced my voice. "Why don't you come and sit down?"

His head shaking became more agitated. "It's not right."

"I know it's not right, and I'm angry too. Sit with me. We can talk about it."

He twisted around. I saw only his back as he bent over the desk. "There's... so much you don't know."

"Then tell me."

"I can't."

"Yes, you can. We're past the point of secrets."

"No one knows. No one is supposed to know. That's why all this started."

"What? Ryder, I don't understand." I went over to him and put my hand on his back. I felt a shudder pass over him. "Look, you're freaking. Just take a minute and breathe."

He didn't seem to have heard me. "I don't blame you for what you did," he forced out, spittle showered the desk. "I would have killed him too! I wanted to— I was going to—"

I was truly getting worried. I had dealt with Ryder in many states, but never like this. "Ryder, calm down. It's okay." I pressed my hand to his cheek and he whipped around, startling a cry out of me. His eyes were huge.

"I wanted to kill her, Val. I was going to do it."

"Kill—"

"That night in the woods."

I stilled as those words struck me. "The woods. You mean the masquerade dance?"

"You saw us." The words were pouring out of him and it didn't seem like he could stop it. "You saw us that night, but it was me with the knife. I thought it was over. She had moved from the prep school to the academy, away from the boys, but then I heard her that night, telling Professor Rossman that she was going to start an outreach center for kids."

"Who was?" My head was spinning; I was doing everything to keep up. "Who moved?"

"I got the knife. I don't know why, but I did. I came back, and I made her come with me to the woods. I was going to do what I should have done so long ago. *Stop her!*"

I took his face in my hands, and he immediately grabbed my wrists, clinging tightly. "But you were there, Val. You weren't supposed to be there, and when that card showed up in your locker, I found out she was more than just a fucking pedophile, she was a Spade."

"Who, Ryder? Who is it?"

He looked me in the eyes as fevered pants warmed the air between us, and he said two words I never expected to hear.

"Scarlett LeBlanc."

Chapter Ten

Ryder and I sat splayed out on the floor. Neither of us had moved for twenty minutes. I didn't know about Ryder, but I was pretty sure what I was feeling matched being run over by a truck—twice.

Scarlett was the person in the woods. Scarlett is a Spade. The kind woman who gave me painting lessons and told me about Walter marked me... and she hurt Ryder.

This time, it was me who reached for his hand. Ryder curled his fingers through mine, and together, we went back to staring at the wall.

Knock. Knock.

"Hey, Ryder." The keypad chimed, signaling they were coming in before either of us could think to do something. "Here's your shaving..." Ezra trailed off as he took us in. I saw his eyes flick down to our clasped hands. "What's going on in here?"

"Get Maverick," Ryder said.

"But—"

"Go."

Ezra didn't argue further and stepped out of the room. When he returned, it was with Maverick and Jaxson in tow.

"What's going on?" asked Jaxson.

Ryder looked across him to Maverick. "She knows."

Maverick's grave expression said it all.

"Hold on." I looked from him to Ryder. "You know too? About the woods?"

"Know what?" Ezra demanded.

"What about the woods?" This came from Jaxson.

"But *they* don't know?" I said to Ryder. "Wait a minute. Is that the real reason you were outside the night of the dance? You were keeping watch?" I addressed this to Maverick.

"Someone want to tell us what's going on?" Ezra sounded pissed now.

"She knows about Scarlett," said Ryder.

Jaxson's eyes popped. "She knows what?! Who the fuck told you that you could—"

"She knows what she did to me," Ryder cut in. "She also saw me try to attack Scarlett in the woods. I was shouting about what she did, and she promised I would regret it if I told anyone. Then we heard Valentina. Scarlett couldn't have known how much she saw or overheard, but she marked her to get rid of her."

"Scarlett's a Spade?" Ezra asked through pale lips. "And you knew that for a whole year and didn't say anything!?"

"What would telling you have done?"

My eyes ping-ponged between the group. It was strange sitting there holding Ryder's hand while the awful truth came out.

"Maverick knew," Ryder went on, "and we've been working on a way to get rid of her without getting us all marked too."

"Argh!" Jaxson shouted. "That's why we were chosen to be Knights. I knew it was too much of a fucking coincidence! I said it!"

"You were right," said Ryder.

"What's this plan? How can you not let us be a part of it?" Ezra spoke up.

"Still working on it," Maverick admitted. "It's hard when we have to play nice."

"She's a Spade," said Jaxson. "For how long? What psycho let that happen?"

"Guys!" My yell brought the noise to an abrupt halt. Four pairs of eyes flew to me as I let go of Ryder and got to my feet. "That's enough. My head is spinning and we'll never make sense of things like this. So here it is: Ryder overheard Scarlett say she was going to start working with young boys again. He lured her to the woods to confront her and I saw. She marked me and tipped Ryder off to her being a Spade. Since then, he and Maverick have been trying to find a way to get rid of her, but what I don't get is why she stopped at marking me if she wanted me gone?"

"Did she stop?" asked Jaxson. "Someone pushed that planter over, Val, and started the fire in your room."

The sentence chilled me to my core. "Scarlett's been trying to kill me."

"She probably couldn't believe her luck when you came into class clearly not knowing who she was," said Ryder, "but that didn't mean she wanted you around to find out. That's how the marks work. They get rid of problems."

"But I'm not going anywhere. She isn't going to force me out of Evergreen so what now?" I fixed on Maverick. "What's your plan?"

Maverick looked to Ryder. "What do you want to do?"

"We need to talk," Jaxson said. "That's what we do."

Ezra nodded. "Agreed. What else have you been keeping from us?"

I opened my mouth.

"Val?" Ryder gripped my shoulder. "You have to go."

"But—"

"I'll find you after, but you need to go now."

I looked around at the four faces and saw they were united. Knights against me.

"Fine."

I left with no more arguments and made the walk back to my dorm. Sofia looked up from my computer when I came in.

"Hey, Val. How did it go? Did you talk with Ryder?"

I looked at her—face open and supportive, and I made up my mind.

"Sofia, there's something I need to tell you..."

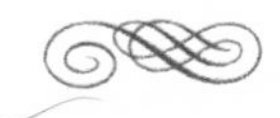

SOFIA STAYED WITH ME for the rest of the weekend. She said it was because she wanted to make sure I was okay, but I think she was shaken up after learning about Adam and who his father was. I didn't tell her about how Benjamin died, Ryder's mom, or the money, but I did feel a weight lift off my shoulders at finally telling her Adam was my son.

I wasn't ashamed of him, and Adam would always know who I was, but other people asked questions when you tell them you gave birth at fourteen. I didn't want questions.

"It feels wrong to have to go back to class like nothing happened," Sofia said as I locked the door behind us. "If you want to sit out, I'll tell administration you're sick."

I shook my head. "No, I'm good. This weekend was emotionally wrecking, but classes will take my mind off of it." Over her head I spotted Kane. "You should go. Have a good day."

We hugged and then she broke off for class. Kane fell in step beside me, and as we walked to homeroom, I thought about the Knights and Ryder. What had they decided? Did Ryder mean it when he said he would come and tell me everything? Had things changed between us?

How could it not after going through something like that and sharing the things we had? I don't know what happens from here, but it can't go back to the way it was.

They were all there when I walked into homeroom. I met all of their eyes, but they were impossible to read. I made the effort of reading from my chem book, but the letters blurred on the page after five minutes. I couldn't focus.

Homeroom let out after thirty long minutes, and I swung by my locker for my notebook.

"Morning, baby."

"Jaxson?" I wrenched my head out as he sidled up next to me. "What's going on? When are we going to talk?"

"Easy." He spared a glance around and landed on Kane. "Can you tell your boy to back up a few steps?"

I did and Kane moved out of earshot.

"We're meeting up tonight," Jaxson said under his breath. "At the cliffs. Nine o'clock. Ezra will pick you up so make sure you shake the guard loose by then."

"Alright. Nine o'clock."

He sauntered off—looking every bit the carefree Jaxson and I envied him. I didn't know how to act now that I knew what Scarlett was. I couldn't have been more thankful that I never had to take her class again.

My mind was in such a fog, I heard about it from Ciara.

"What are you doing? You're measuring everything out wrong."

"Sorry." I put the beaker down. "Maybe you should do this part."

"You said you weren't going to mess with my grade."

"I'm not. That will mess up my grade too."

We fell quiet as I cleaned out the beaker and redid the measurements.

"Val?"

"It's two point six ounces."

"Val, why are you here?"

"What?" I squinted at her through the goggles.

"Why stay here after everything—"

I cut her off with a groan. "I swear if one more person asks me that. I'm here because I gave up a lot to be. I've earned my place here, more than the assholes who tried to drive me out, so I'm not leaving until I get my diploma. Does that answer your question?"

Ciara looked blown away by my reply. I wasn't intending for it to come out as forcefully as it did, but I had been having an intense... life.

"Yes, sorry."

We fell silent again and went back to our work.

I PACED UP AND DOWN the floor of my front hall that night. Every five seconds I looked at my phone to check the time.

It's 9:01. Where is he?

No sooner had I finished the thought than there was a knock at the door. I pulled it open on Ezra.

"You ready?"

"I am." I stepped out and he turned to go without pausing for chitchat. I locked up and hurried to catch up to him. "You're pissed at me."

"You have the whole school thinking I beat you," he answered without slowing his stride. "Pissed is putting it lightly."

"Does the school think that? Last I checked, everyone is happy to believe I did it to myself."

Ezra's eyes were even darker at night. He narrowed them at me, and the white disappeared until I was looking through an endless abyss. "My mom doesn't believe it. She sent me to anger management over the break. You need to tell her the truth."

"I could do that. I *would* do that. If I thought you were sorry."

"Sorry? Sorry for what?"

"If you have to ask that, then we have no more to talk about."

"Moon—"

"I'm done, Ezra."

No more words passed between us as we stepped into the woods. Ezra had a flashlight to show our way, but he stepped with such assurance, I figured he could do without the light. I hadn't gotten many invitations to the cliffs since I was marked, and the one I did get was a disaster.

A niggle of fear curdled in my stomach. What if this was another cruel trick?

A glow broke through the tree line and soon we were stepping out into the clearing. Jaxson, Ryder, and Maverick looked up from their spots around the fire when we appeared. Somehow they had gotten chairs out here, and there was a fifth one for me.

Ezra sat down next to Maverick which left me between Ryder and Jaxson. I spoke up the minute my butt hit the seat. "What's your plan to take down Scarlett?"

The boys shared a look.

"What? You said you would tell me." I made to get up. "If this is a trick—"

Ryder grabbed my hand and pulled me back down. "We'll tell you, but there's something we want to know first."

I scanned their faces. "What is it?"

"The stuff you did this year... how did you pull it off?"

"Why is that important?"

Maverick leaned forward. "We don't have a right to ask, but we need you to trust us. How did you do it?"

I stared at him for a long time, but he held my gaze, not looking away. They didn't have a right to ask me to trust them, but...

Jaxson saved your life and Ryder shared his assault with you. They may have bought an ounce of faith.

Only an ounce.

"Okay," I began. "I hired a hacker to get in Jaxson's phone."

"The same one who infected my computer?" asked Maverick.

"Yep."

"That means they're good," Ezra murmured.

Ryder piped up. "What about the Evergreen Gone Wild video?"

"Button cam. Always recording and saving straight to my phone."

"Smart," said Maverick.

"I thought so."

"And are you done now?" My attention was drawn to Ryder. The fire flicked in his eyes and it was impossible to look away. "Have you gotten your revenge against everyone?"

"Not everyone. There are still a few people on my list."

"Who?"

"Why do you want to know?"

"Because we'll take care of them for you... if you take down Scarlett."

I blinked at him. I couldn't have heard that right. "Take care of them for me?"

"Whatever you were planning, we'll take it on—the risk, the blame, the consequences. We can handle it."

"But what we can't do," Jaxson continued, "is get near Scarlett without her thinking something is up. Ryder has already tried to attack her; she won't take chances with us."

Maverick picked up the thread. "She won't be the same with you. She thinks you trust her. You hang out in her classroom all the time. Scarlett won't think twice about you walking in there alone."

I nodded along. All of this made sense, except for one. "Why do you think you have to carry out my revenge to convince me?"

"Because we won't be able to protect you," Ryder said, "and this woman most likely tried to kill you twice."

I bit my lip. That was a good point.

"We have a plan, and we'll tell you all of it right now. Just let us know if we have a deal."

I didn't let them rush me. I took my time thinking about it, and kept coming up with one thing. They were offering to help me take out everyone on my list. How could I say no? "I'll agree on one condition," I announced. "You tell me why this is so important to you."

Ryder frowned. "Val, you know why."

"Not you, Ryder." I swept over the other three faces. "Why are you guys doing this?"

Ryder rose out of his seat. "You don't have to—"

"Because it wasn't just Ryder." His soft reply was almost lost in the sound of the crackling fire. Ezra looked at me, and for the first time, I understood what was in his eyes. "She molested me too."

"And me," came from Maverick.

Jaxson didn't say it. He just held up a hand.

The familiar tightness stirred in my chest. It was hard to breathe, but this time it wasn't for me.

"Alright. I'll do it."

"UM... VAL?"

"Yes?"

"This is weird, right?"

I looked at the four boys casually taking up the available spaces in my room. Maverick crouched on the floor, searching through my secret suitcase. Ryder and Ezra were at my desk, and Jaxson had boldly hopped on my bed with the notebook I had been using for my plans.

"Yes," I replied. "This is definitely weird."

"I need to talk to you." Sofia grabbed my arm and hauled me off. She shut the bathroom door on the bizarro world outside. "What is going on? Why are they here?"

After what she just walked in on, there was no way I could get away with not explaining, but I had no clue where to begin.

"So Ryder and I—"

Got into it on the roof and I was almost sent plunging to my death.

"—talked," I finished. "We talked and got everything out. The war between us is over."

She goggled at me. "Val, are you serious? But what about the things he's done to you. Not only when you were marked, but before you came here. How could you put that aside?"

"It's hard to explain, but we... understand each other more now."

She looked back toward the door. "Why are they here?"

"We made a deal." I placed my hands on the countertop and hopped up. "They are going to help me get back at Isabella and Natalie if I help them take down the Spades."

"Hold on. *They* want to take down the Spades? Why?"

I pushed down the surge of rage that followed the thought of Scarlett. "They don't like them any more than we do."

Sofia held out her hands and I took them immediately. "What if they're playing you again?"

I thought of us sitting around the dying fire while the boys told me something they had never shared with anyone but each other. "I still don't fully trust them, but this time I know they aren't lying. This isn't a trick."

"Okay." She squeezed my fingers. "I trust you so if you say they're for real; I'll go along with it."

"Thank you."

Maverick looked up when we came out of the bathroom. My tiny button cam was nestled in his palm. "Valentina, was your hacker able to get into the school's network?"

I shook my head. "You should be proud of your dad. He's too good."

"So good I can't get in either and I learned from him. He..." Maverick trailed off as he reached in and pulled something out of the suitcase. My eyes bugged at the green metal piece between his fingertips.

"I don't know how that got in there." I darted across the room and plucked it from his hand. It went sailing over my shoulder. "So what were you saying about the network?"

"It doesn't matter now." I wish I could tell what was going on in Maverick's head, but he was even harder to read than Ezra. "We'll figure out the rest later."

"First," said Jaxson. He tossed the notebook to the side. "Natalie Bard."

Suddenly all the boys were packing up my things and getting ready to leave.

"What are you going to do to her?" I asked them.

Ezra held up one of my secret phones. "Exactly what you would have done: total and complete emotional annihilation." There was an edge to his voice. He and I may have understood each other, but he wasn't close to forgiving me for coming between him and his mother.

"And my phone is going to help you do that?"

He slipped it into his pocket without replying.

"Are you going to the chess tournament?" My eyes slid off Ezra's face to Ryder. It was amazing how perfectly he had put together his mask. The raw, naked pain of the guy I met in his bedroom was gone; the Ryder Shea I knew was back... with a few exceptions.

"Yes, I am."

"Then make sure you get a front row seat."

"You're going to get her then? But those tournaments are locked down tight, and thanks to the headmaster, it's even worse." I glanced at Sofia. "We haven't been able to see a way around it."

"There's a way." Ryder jerked his head and the guys headed for the door. "Just be there."

They blew out of my room in a haze of expensive cologne.

Sofia shook her head. "Yep. This is weird."

I WAS COUNTING THE days until the tournament, but with my own stuff going on I couldn't obsess about Natalie or the Knights too much.

I landed on the mat with a smack that made Yvette hiss.

"You okay, Valentina?"

Groaning, I forced myself to my feet and shook it off. "Yes. I put a little too much jump in that flip and knocked myself off balance."

"Well, if you know what you did wrong, try again and do it right this time."

I nodded and Yvette started my music again. At my cue, I threw myself into the routine. With the 104 Hot FM Solo competition coming up, Yvette and I had been practicing after regular club meetings.

I ran it through perfectly and couldn't help but smile when the music stopped. Yvette was smiling too.

"Nicely done, Valentina. You're set to win this thing."

I laughed breathlessly. "You say that, but you're still going to make me do it two more times."

"Three actually." Yvette grabbed my water bottle off the bench and tossed it to me. "Five-minute break then we'll go again."

I plopped down on the mat in blessed relief. Yvette was a great coach, but she did not mess around. She was infected with the Evergreen Academy need to be the best and she was expecting me or Isabella to win this competition—and that winner will be me.

"Val?" Yvette strode over to me and sat on the mat. "I've talked to Isabella about this and now I'd like to know your opinion."

I lowered the bottle. "Is everything okay?"

"Yes. It's nothing bad. It's that usually we only open it up for students to join us and watch us compete when we have big team competitions like nationals or regionals. We missed our chance for that, but the headmaster offered to let the school support us for the 104 Hot FM contest. Students who choose will ride the bus with us to Martindale and watch you and Isabella perform... unless you don't want that." She gave me a surprisingly sad smile. "I know you've had a hard time, and if the students will be more of a distraction than a support, I will tell him it's not happening."

I took my time thinking about it. The only time I didn't feel marked was when I was dancing. When I was in that place where the music and my body connected and the darkness couldn't touch me. I didn't want the Evergreen kids to take that away.

"It's okay," I finally said. "They can come. I'm strong. I won't break. It's taken me too long to realize that."

The smile morphed into one that didn't make me want to cry. "You are strong, Valentina."

Bang!

I looked toward the door as Isabella marched inside. She planted herself in front of us with narrowed eyes lasered on me. "Why is she here? Mother was supposed to call you about the new practice schedule."

"And as I told your mother," Yvette said as she got to her feet. "I cannot block every afternoon to practice with you alone. Valentina is also in the competition."

She frowned. "But I can only work with Vibes on the weekends and we have to make sure my routine is perfect. I thought we wanted to win this thing."

"You both have an excellent chance of winning this contest and we will make sure of it at practice *twice* a week. That will be more than enough time to prepare."

Isabella did not look mollified. She put her hands on her lithe hips and I took that as my cue to get up and grab my towel. When she hopped on the complain train, she didn't stop anytime soon. Something I learned from enduring being on the team with her.

"This wouldn't happen in a ballet production," I heard her say. "Principals are given the time and attention they need to prepare. I'll be auditioning for Victoria in *The Red Shoes* and when I get the part, my instructors will—"

"—do what is necessary to prepare you for the role," Yvette finished. "Just like they should and just like I will. You need to trust me, Isabella, but more than that, you need to remember *this is not ballet*."

I peeked at them around my towel, eyes wide.

"You're on my team. These are my rules." She leveled a finger at the door. "Now, leave. This is Valentina's practice time."

She didn't go quietly, but eventually Isabella stomped out and Yvette turned her stern expression on me.

"Alright. Three more times, Valentina. Get to it."

I hid a smile. "Yes, Coach."

YVETTE WENT TO BATTLE for me, but by the end of the school week I knew I was ready. I wasn't going to leave that competition with anything other than first place.

I polished off my turkey, avocado, and goat cheese panini and stood with the rest of my class when the bell rang. Third period had been canceled for us to watch Natalie Bard compete for her title as chess grand master.

Sofia caught my eye as we shuffled to the competition room. I read her unease like a tattoo on her face. I had no clue what the

Knights were going to do to Natalie and that didn't sit right with her. Sofia wanted them to stick to our rules, but Ryder hadn't responded when she cornered him about it. We both knew how ruthless they could be.

I stepped through the double doors and our eyes found each other instantly. Ryder stood just before the stage. Above his head, Natalie schmoozed with a bunch of people I didn't recognize.

Ryder looked from me to the seats in front of him. I got the hint. He wanted me front row and center.

I made my way over there and Sofia fell in beside me.

"I don't like this," she said out of the corner of her mouth. "Those boys are demons. Beautiful, sexy, evil, rip-your-heart-out-and-drink-the-blood demons."

"True, but Natalie is the same. The girl tripped me on the track and took half the skin on my back off."

"She's awful, but we don't know what they're going to do."

I kept my eyes fixed ahead as we traveled down the aisle. "You told them the rules. I'm sure they'll stick with them."

"Are you?"

Not even a little bit. Beautiful, sexy, evil demons tend not to be predictable. I have no clue what is going to happen.

I passed Ryder on my way to my seat, feeling his eyes on me the whole way. Sofia plopped down a couple of seats away. When I looked for Ryder again, he was gone, so I turned to Natalie. She looked relaxed—in her element. By her side was an older man with a scruffy beard, twice as many piercings, and a face that said he was Natalie's father.

Headmaster Evergreen stepped out onto the stage and that was the cue for the others to find their place.

"Good afternoon, Evergreen students and honored guests. Many have traveled great distances to be here today and see some of the brightest strategic minds of our time compete for the title of grand master. Let's welcome our contestants."

I listened with half an ear while he rattled off names and introductions. Behind him, the screen lowered and staff fussed about setting up the table.

"Now to our contestants," Evergreen continued. "In order of rank, you will play against Miss Bard. There will be two designated bathroom breaks and both times you will be escorted to and from the room to ensure there is no cheating."

Wow. This is serious, I thought as I took in the black-suited individuals posted at different spots in the auditorium. How could the Knights have possibly pulled anything off in here? It was locked down too tight.

"Let's begin."

Natalie rose from her seat and took her place before the chess set. The projector flicked on and we were treated to an overhead view of the game, allowing us to see every move made. Her first challenger sat across from her and the tournament began.

Want to know something? Chess matches are boring as hell.

I slipped into a coma about thirty minutes in and didn't rouse until a mic tap jerked me to reality.

Evergreen cleared his throat. "Now for the first break. Contestants may use the bathroom or get a snack. Students must remain seated."

My eyes stuck to Natalie as she trailed a black-suit to the double doors. No one except the staff was allowed to be alone with the contestants.

The break lasted ten minutes and soon everyone returned to take their places. I knew next to nothing about chess, but that didn't prevent me from seeing Natalie was killing it. There were only three challengers left and they were looking nervous.

"Players, take your seats."

Natalie sat before the chess set and a boy a few years older than her. They shook hands as I tried to keep my eyes open.

"Natalie Bard will be playing against Gael Erbach," Evergreen said. "Mr. Erbach is—"

Bang!

"Hold the competition!"

Evergreen swung toward the door. "What is the meaning of this?"

Two black-suits marched down the row. "We must stop the match. This was found in the girl's bathroom."

Black-suit held something up in her hand and I squinted for a better look.

Is that—?

"A cell phone," she said. "It was cleverly hidden in the paper dispenser, and from what we can tell—"

My eyes popped. *My phone? That's my phone!*

"—this phone belongs to Miss Bard."

"What?!" A crash sounded in the auditorium as Natalie's chair toppled over. "That's not mine!"

Evergreen looked from Natalie to the woman dumbfounded. "Phones are not allowed on this campus and Miss Bard is one of our top students. There must be some mistake."

"There is no mistake. The bathroom was swept before she went in and we're certain there was no phone. We checked it and found her photo on the home screen. More importantly, an examination of the phone revealed a search of the Tarrasch Defense and the Folkestone Variation." The woman lowered her hand and pinned Natalie with a look that bordered on disgust. "Natalie Bard is disqualified for cheating."

All hell broke loose.

"It wasn't me! That's not mine!" Natalie shot forward, knocking the table. It tipped over and fell with a crash that elicited screams. Natalie made a run for the woman until her father intercepted her. "I didn't do it!"

"That's enough!" Evergreen roared. "Settle down! Students, leave the auditorium now!"

It was chaos getting everyone out and calming Natalie down. I stumbled out of there in a daze, Ezra's words echoing in my mind.

"Exactly what you would have done: total and complete emotional annihilation."

THE WEEKEND FLEW BY in a shower of whispers and disbelief. Monday saw Natalie missing from homeroom. Her father ended up taking her out of school while they fought the decision to take away her grand master title. It was becoming a mess of lawyers, investigations, and Natalie's name dragged through the media.

"Normally people wouldn't care about some chess tournament," Sofia said from her spot at my desk. She had snuck away from the cafeteria to eat dinner with me. She had asked a few times why we didn't meet on the roof anymore but I didn't have an answer that she would like. "But this is the latest scandal in the Evergreen Gone Wild saga and the press is hitting it hard."

"She did an interview for the Evergreen Post. She's saying she was sabotaged."

Sofia swiveled around to face me. "She was."

I shook my head as I rested my tray on my lap. "I don't know exactly how they did it, but I'm guessing it involved some Maverick hacker magic and sneaking into the bathroom at the right time. They're good. I might have gotten Alex to help me with the phone, but getting it into the girl's room with security all over the place would have been too tricky."

Sofia was quiet for a moment. "You sound impressed."

"They did what we wanted *and* they did it by our rules." I leaned back until she was partly obscured by the bedpost. "Now, there's only Isabella."

Sofia pushed the chair back until she found me again. "I don't think you'll need them for Isabella. You'll have total and complete emotional annihilation covered when you beat her in the competition this Saturday."

I scooped in a mouthful of honey garlic shrimp and cauliflower rice. "She thinks she's got me beat, and with Vibes Taranto as her teacher, she's got reason to be smug."

Sofia laughed. "What was that? Smibes Balanto? Wanna swallow that first?"

Giggling, I did as she asked and tried again. "She's got a hip-hop legend choreographing her moves and she's not even kind of worried about me."

"That will make it all the more satisfying when you beat her." Sofia got up and joined me on the bed. "Is your mom coming to the contest?"

"She can't. A friend is going out of town and asked her to babysit. She's sat for me and Adam so many times; she didn't want to say no. But the contest is being streamed live so she's going to watch me."

"Well, so am I. I'll be front row—"

I opened my mouth.

"—and don't try to tell me not to go." She smacked my thigh. "Of course I'm going to be there."

"Ouch," I grumbled. "I didn't even say it."

"You were thinking it." Sofia snatched my coconut cookie off my plate. "Now you've lost this. See what you do?"

I was stuck between laughing and wanting my cookie back. In the end, I tackled her and she guffawed so hard the cookie came back up. We were in tears—cracking up like we hadn't done in a while, but one thought remained in the back of my mind.

It won't be enough to beat her in the competition. I pressed my hand to my chest when Sofia turned away, feeling the tightness I knew well. *Not after she posted sex flyers of me all over the school. Not after she dug her nails in my arm, trapping me while Jaxson told the world what happened to me. That would never be enough.*

My hand curled into a fist, pressing harder. *They better have something good planned for her because I'm all too happy to handle Isabella Bruno myself.*

Chapter Eleven

My duffle bag flew off my shoulder and crashed to the ground.

"Watch it, Moon!"

Eyes narrowing into slits, I didn't give Natalie the satisfaction of seeing me rub the spot where she ran into me. She had come to school that Thursday ten times as mean, and she was directing all that bitch energy at me.

"What the fuck is your problem?" I spat back. "How many times do I have to tell you I *didn't* get you disqualified?!"

Natalie swung around. Her fists were balled up like she wanted to bury them in my face. Behind her, the bus taking us to Martindale gleamed in the blazing sun. I'd rather not throw down before the biggest competition of my life, but this girl was pushing it.

"I know it was you!" She advanced on me until she was in my face. "That phone *wasn't* mine!"

I folded my arms. "You know for a supposedly smart girl; you're acting bat-shit stupid. When did I plant the phone, Natalie? I was sitting in front of you the whole time!"

"You put it there before the tournament!"

"Security checked before the tournament!"

"I know it was you!"

"Prove it!"

"Ladies! That is enough!" Yvette shoved her way between us, sending me and Natalie stumbling away. She shot me a furious look. "Valentina, you do not have time for this. Get your things and get on the bus. As for you"—she turned on Natalie—"you are not coming with us. Go back inside."

"But I—"

"No buts. I won't have you causing problems with my dancer when she needs to focus. The school has been suffering under too much *embarrassment* and it's past time we've had some positive attention."

Natalie flushed bright red, but she didn't back down. "I want to see Isabella compete."

"Tough." Yvette swooped down and snagged my bag off the floor. My arm was next. "Inside. Now."

Yvette dragged me off leaving a steaming Natalie in our wake. A small crowd gathered in front of the door to the bus. Not many students chose to come with us, but the entire dance team was here along with Sofia, Paisley, and the Knights.

I met Ryder's gaze for all of two seconds before looking away. Things felt even weirder now than they did when we hated each other.

Yvette clapped. "Okay, everyone. We're leaving in five minutes. Thank you all for coming out to support the team and our contestants. That said, let me warn you the headmaster has promised severe repercussions for anyone who makes trouble." She swept her eyes over the group. "Which *no one* is going to do... correct?"

Nods and murmurs of agreement went around. Yvette accepted it and finally let us board the bus.

I climbed up last and paused next to the driver. Isabella had taken up court in the middle of the bus with Airi at her side. I could hear her bragging about her routine above the noise. Sofia sat up front next to Eric and Paisley. Sitting with her was never going to happen but the two of them made sure.

I kept going until I landed on them in the back. The Knights took up the entire last row and the empty seats around them spoke to the barrier that existed between them and the regular students. I picked up my feet and walked to the back.

"...so easy. People pretend like hip-hop is hard but I'd like to see them balance their entire body on blistered toes." Isabella's voice grated on me as I passed by her group. "This contest is no big deal. Afterward, I'm going to my audition for the Red Shoes so we'll make that two wins in one day."

"Can't expect anything less from the leader of the Diamonds," someone replied, "and people thought *she* was going to take your place..."

I tuned the rest out as I made for the row in front of the Knights. I swung around and took my seat without looking at them.

Evergreen is beautiful. The campus lay before me large and magnificent, dwarfing the horizon. *If only it wasn't as much of a mask as the one we all wear.*

"Are you planning something?" I asked. My eyes were fixed out of the window. "For Isabella at the contest?"

"Don't worry about it." Jaxson's reply drifted through the seats. "We'll take care of her; you bring home the gold."

"It's the painted plastic actually, but you don't need to keep me out of this. I want to know."

"You will know. After we're done, everyone will know."

Jaxson didn't say the conversation was over, but the message came through loud and clear. I could have pushed it but with her only a few feet away it wasn't the best time.

The ride to Martindale was only an hour, but it was made longer by having nothing to do or anyone to talk to. I heard the boys behind me laughing and yukking it up as they always did and Jaxson's words were pulled from my mind.

"Sometimes things happen—big things. And it binds people together so freaking tight that you have to be friends... because no one else will ever understand you like they do."

Trees soon gave way to red-brick buildings and bustling centers as we found ourselves in the city of Martindale. That this was a wealthy place was obvious by the designer-clad couples pushing miniature dogs in strollers and the sports cars that honked at our bus before swerving off. Posters and banners for the competition began to take up every light post and storefront and I knew we were close.

The driver turned onto a narrow street and the building loomed before us. A bubbling energy that filled me whenever I danced made an early appearance.

Finally. Let's do this.

The bus dropped us off at the entrance. The group made it two feet before a woman with a clipboard descended on us fast. I pulled up quick before she ran into me.

"You must be the Evergreen crew!" She grabbed my hand and about shook it out of its socket. "We're excited to have you." She peeked at her board. "I see you have two dancers in the contest."

"That's right." Yvette stepped out in front of me. "Isabella Bruno and Valentina Moon."

"Got 'em." She flapped a hand. "My name is Kiara and I'll take over from here. Coach, you and the rest of your group can find your seats. We have you second row, right in the center. Ladies, follow me."

Kiara took off at a brisk pace. I hurried to catch up with her as she led us through a cavernous room. Awe made me tilt my head all the way back to the glass ceiling. The sun shone brightly on the platform that would be my stage and surrounding it were the stands.

Kiara led us past all of that to a side hallway. People streamed around us, rushing in and out of marked doors looking as nervous as I felt.

"It's intense back here."

I almost tripped. "Jaxson?" I swung my head around and there he was, trailing us like it was no big deal. "What are you doing back here?"

He said nothing—just tossed me a wink.

"This is your dressing room." Kiara had stopped in front of a door marked Evergreen Academy. "You can get dressed and do some last-minute practice in here. If you want to watch the competition; you are more than welcome. If not, I will come and get you when it's your turn."

"Thank you." I was highly aware of Jaxson's presence at my back. Isabella looked at him curiously, but didn't comment. She turned her attention on me when I stepped forward.

"Actually"—her hand flashed out to block my way—"we can't share the same dressing room. We're competing against each other. I won't have her seeing my routine."

Kiara blinked. "Against each other? But you're on the same team."

The looks on our faces must have said it all because Kiara plastered the smile back on her face. "Okay, okay. Not a problem." Her brows snapped together as she consulted her clipboard. "There are no more dressing rooms available, but there are single bathrooms that you could—"

"Good. She'll take that." Isabella marched inside and slammed the door behind her.

Kiara's smile twitched as she turned it on me. "Let me show you to the bathroom."

"Thanks."

She led us down another hallway—yes, us. I hadn't managed to shake Jaxson loose, but I was trusting there must be a reason he was sticking close.

"Here you are. Do you need anything before I go? Water? A snack?"

"No, thank you." Kiara took off leaving us alone. "Is this about whatever you're going to do to Isabella?"

"No."

"Then why are you following me?"

"Wanted to wish you luck." Jaxson slid his hands out of his pockets and put them on my waist. He pulled me in. "No one can dance like you, baby. The rest of those jokers don't stand a chance. You got that?"

His hands burned through the fabric of my shirt, radiating heat through my body. His touch was so addicting. I couldn't resist the day we spent in my bed, and it wasn't any easier now. A smile tugged at my lips. "I got it."

"Good." His grin turned wicked in a blink. "Then how about a kiss for good luck?"

Jaxson leaned in, eyes fluttering shut, and I stomped on the butterflies quick enough to clap my hand on his face.

"Why don't you grab your seat, playboy? Save that mouth for cheering me on."

Jaxson's laugh made his lips brush against my palm. "Whatever you say."

He backed away, eyes on me the whole time, until he rounded the corner and disappeared.

I rubbed my hand absentmindedly against my pants as I let myself into the bathroom. It tingled where his lips touched.

It took me a second to come back down, but eventually I shook myself and opened my duffle. The outfit I chose was simple—baggy black pants and a ripped green top—but it was easy to move in. My makeup I applied with a light hand and my final touch was to put my hair in a ponytail.

There was no way I was sitting out in this bathroom and not seeing the competition. The stands were filling up fast, but I spotted our yellow uniforms easily in the crowd. There was a free seat in front of Sofia and Eric. I sat down as Kiara stepped to the middle of the platform.

"Hello, everyone, and welcome to 104 Hot FM's hip-hop contest." Cheers went up all around me. "We've got some great dancers showing their stuff today. We're going to kick things off in a few minutes, but first, I want to introduce you to our judges."

I tuned her out as she rattled off the names of the five people sitting off to the side. *I can do this. I can win this. I will win this. I have to. Isabella is going to find out what it's like to be a loser today.*

"—get this thing started!"

Music blasted through the speakers jolting me back. The first dancer ran out to the platform and the contest was underway. To say there was some serious talent here was putting it lightly. The music was on point, the dancers hit every step and beat, and the crowd was going wild—me included. I got lost in the performances, forgetting about Isabella and all of it.

This is what I loved about dancing—the energy, the rhythm, the way it pulled me out of the darkness and made me feel like I could breathe again.

"Whoo! That was amazing, wasn't it?" The crowd cheered the contestant off the stage as Kiara came on the scene. "Now for our next dancer... Isabella Bruno!"

"This should be interesting." Eric's voice floated over the noise and reached my ears. I had a feeling all the Evergreen students were on the edge of their seats for this performance.

Isabella trotted out with her head high. She went with a pink leotard under a loose tank. Stepping onto the stage, she moved to the middle and struck a pose. After a beat, the music came on and she was off.

Wow.

I wish I could have fought the thought, but that was exactly the word Isabella deserved. She had taken a chance to mix ballet with hip-hop, classical with new school, and it paid off in a big way. She was unlike any of the dancers who came before. Isabella glided from move to move, from pop to lock, effortlessly. When the music faded the roar from the crowd was deafening.

Isabella gave a small bow. On her way back up, she looked right at me and smirked.

"Wonderful! Let's give another round of applause for Isabella!" Kiara let the crowd go on for a bit then jogged out onto the stage. "Now we have one more contestant representing Evergreen Academy—"

I took a deep breath. *This is it.*

"—Valentina Moon!"

I was up. I streaked across to the platform and shook Kiara's hand to hearty cheers from the crowd, but nothing from my class.

The Evergreen kids looked at me with everything from disinterest to hostility. Most of them didn't care about my win—didn't think it could happen.

My music came on as I pushed them from my mind. My cue pounded through the speakers and I was gone.

The song I chose was a Latin/hip-hop mix. Those were the songs Mom and I would dance to the nights she let me stay up past my bedtime—just the two of us having fun together. They were the songs I sang to a newborn Adam when he rested on my chest. His tiny little head tucked contentedly under my neck. It was the songs that made me want to dance. That made me think I could one day smile again even in the worst times of my life.

"And what will make it go away? What's going to put you back together?"

The song shifted tempo and I spun, letting the tears that had been clinging to my lashes fly.

I'm going to put me back together, I thought to the question I was never able to answer before. *I'll never be so broken that I can't find my way back. For Mom and my son... and for me... I'll be okay.*

My song neared its end and on the final word, I flipped. This was the flip I had struggled with in practice. Half the time I ended up flat on my back, but this time I knew it was perfect. My feet glided over my head as if carried by the air.

I landed with a smack and threw my hands up. The cheers from the crowd rattled the building. They battled against my eardrums as I jogged off to my bathroom. Tears flowed freely now, but they were the good kind. The kind that came with healing.

"LET'S BRING OUR CONTESTANTS back out here!"

I followed the line of people out to the stage. This was it. Fifteen competitors but only three trophies. Isabella stood at my right. Her back was ramrod straight and head held high as we looked out onto the audience.

Kiara walked in front of us with her ever-present clipboard. "In third place," she began, "give it up for Patrice Margot of Foxhill High!"

Patrice lapped it up, pumping his fists as he ran out to get his trophy.

"In second place—"

My entire body went rigid, firming up tighter than a bowstring.

"—give it up for... Isabella Bruno!"

"What?!"

Isabella's scream sent me rocking back. If she was in second place, did that mean—

"And the winner of the 104 Hot FM Hip-Hop contest is Valentina Moon of Evergreen Academy!"

There were screams. Some of it was Isabella, but a lot of it was me. I ran out and scooped a laughing Kiara in a hug before I could get a hold of myself.

"Congratulations, Valentina," she said. "You deserve it."

I couldn't believe it. I stumbled to my dressing room/bathroom in a fog, clutching my trophy like it would disappear. It wasn't only about the contest. I had won more than just a competition today. I felt lighter than I had in months.

I pushed through into the bathroom. A hand caught the door before it could swing shut.

"Shit, girl!" Jaxson cried as he burst in. "That was insane!"

I laughed. Bubbles were forming in my stomach and spreading till they filled me up.

"But I knew you were going to win." His eyes were shining, cheeks flushed. He looked genuinely happy for me. "Bella was good, but you—"

Clang!

The trophy slipped through my fingertips. I was on him before it hit the ground. Our lips crashed together in an explosion that lit my nerves aflame.

Jaxson staggered back, hitting the doorframe as I wrapped my legs around his thighs. His recovery was quick. In the next breath, our positions were reversed and he was pressing me against the door.

"Yes," he breathed against my lips. "Finally."

I shivered as those two words penetrated my core. I had wondered what it would be like to kiss Jaxson Van Zandt but this came nowhere close to what I could have imagined. I felt like I was at the mercy of a hurricane. A force wild and untamed, and there was nothing I could do to hold it back.

So I didn't try.

Our lips locked in a feverish battle as I ran my hands down his chest, and then finally under his shirt. I might have kept going if our lower halves weren't melded together, grinding in a way that ripped moans from my throat.

Jaxson broke our kiss and traveled down my throat, kissing and nipping as he went. "You don't know how long I've wanted to do this, baby."

Baby took on a whole new meaning at that moment. I laughed. "Yes, I do. You've been hitting on me since the second we met."

His tongue swiped against the sensitive skin of my throat and I bit back a cry. All of these sensations were so new to me. Sex the way it should be.

"I got a little worried there when you said you didn't want me slobbering on you." His fingers dug into my thighs as he ground harder.

"Jaxson," I moaned.

"I hope I'm not too small for you."

Heat flooded my cheeks at the memory of us bare-assed in the broom closet. Jaxson was the furthest thing from small. It would be so easy for me to undress him and do things right.

Am I ready for that?

Jaxson captured my lips again and all my thoughts swept away. I grabbed the hem of his shirt and tugged, fighting to get it over his head.

Knock. Knock. Knock.

"Uhh... Val?"

We froze.

"Just to let you know," said my best friend, "these doors aren't actually that thick...."

I ripped my lips off Jaxson. "What?"

"We can hear everything—"

We?!

"—and the bus is going to leave soon so—"

I didn't hear the rest as I clambered off Jaxson. My cheeks were on fire while I raced to grab my things.

"You go," he said as he moved to the side. "I need a minute."

"But we have to..."

I trailed off when Jaxson looked down. The clear bulge in his pants made me blush even harder. Any more of this and I would pass out from all the blood rushing to my cheeks.

"Right. Okay." I hurried out of the bathroom and ran right into "we."

Ryder stood at Sofia's side. His face was expressionless as he gazed at me. "Only one more to go. Thought you'd like to see the fireworks."

For a minute I didn't know what he was talking about, then it dawned on me. It was time to cross Isabella's name off the list.

I hesitated. "About that—"

"Come on, Val." Sofia grabbed my hand. "We can finally end this."

But I think I've already ended it.

I let her tug me along. Together we followed Ryder outside to the pavement. A crowd had formed before the parking lot and it didn't take me long to realize why.

"Tires slashed?!" Isabella bellowed. "How does that happen?!"

I let go of Sofia's hand and skirted the crowd until the situation laid out before me. Isabella stood before a sleek silver car, shouting at a man in a suit. Looking past her, I could see the sad deflated tires that caused her anger.

"Where were you?!"

"I was in the car, Miss Bruno," he replied calmly. "I'm afraid I didn't see who did it."

"This is unacceptable! I have to be at my audition in an hour!"

"I have called for a backup car but it won't be here in time."

"Then find me something that will!"

"Let's go, everyone." Yvette stepped into my line of sight. "Evergreen students on the bus."

Isabella turned on our coach. "Yvette! Yvette, you have to make the bus driver take me to the audition."

"Not possible," she said without skipping a beat. "He is to take us to and from the competition and nowhere else. We aren't losing our jobs because you have car trouble."

"But—!"

"I will call you a cab, and phone your mother to let her know of the situation. That's the best I can do."

She got up in Yvette's face. "I can't miss this audition. The director doesn't open the doors for anyone after time has started. I will lose my chance to dance Victoria!"

"Everyone." Yvette addressed us as she dialed, not even looking at Isabella. "On the bus now."

This didn't seem like the right time to argue with her. We tromped onto the bus, leaving Isabella screeching in our wake.

SUNDAY NIGHT SOFIA and I crossed the courtyard with our dinner. Kane was on our heels as usual.

"Did you hear what Eric said when we were in line?"

"I heard him mention Isabella," I said. "Did he say what happened after we left?"

"Yvette called her a taxi, but it took like twenty minutes to get there. They didn't come close to making it in time for the audition and she lost her chance at the role."

I whistled. "Something tells me Mother Bruno wasn't pleased."

"You have no idea. She pulled her off the dance team."

"What?" I stopped dead in front of the babbling fountain. "Our dance team?"

"Yep. From what Paisley overheard, she was raging at her not only for losing the contest, but that it was her mixing with *that kind of crowd* that wound up with her tires slashed and her being late. She doesn't want her wasting any more time on a lesser form of dance."

"I see where Isabella gets her lovely personality." Shaking our heads, we kept going toward my dorm.

"You know everyone is talking about you beating her. She's the leader of the Diamonds. This changes everything."

"I know."

Lesson Number Two: There is a hierarchy in Evergreen, and it matters.

"Does that make me leader now?" I asked half-jokingly.

"If you weren't marked, definitely. But since you are..." She trailed off as we both noticed the figure before my door. Ezra stepped out of the shadows.

"Give us a minute," I said to both Sofia and Kane.

"Tonight," Ezra began by way of greeting. He took my arm and pulled me further to the side. "Meet us at the cliffs tonight. We took care of Natalie and Isabella. Now it's time for Scarlett. We want you to do it tomorrow."

"Tomorrow?"

Darkness flitted across Ezra's eyes. "She's dangerous. Waiting only gives her another chance to hurt someone... or you. What if Jaxson isn't there the next time?"

My hands squeezed down on my tray. He was right. There was no good reason to wait.

"Tonight. I'll be there."

Chapter Twelve

I couldn't focus at all in my classes the next day, and not only because I had barely gotten any sleep. The five of us had gone over the plan again and again until the fire burned down. The final bell rang to end the day, but instead of going to Scarlett's class, my legs carried me to the bathroom.

Breathing deep, I splashed cold water on my face.

"You know what to do," I whispered at my dripping reflection. "Let's end this."

I tried again. I left the bathroom and my eyes locked on the door at the end of the hall. The faint *squeak, squeak* of my leather shoes joined the chorus of my racing heart. These things had never seemed so loud to me as they did right then.

"Kane?"

"Yes, Miss Moon."

"I'm going to go in alone, but stay close, okay?"

"Always."

That one word comforted me enough to open the door.

"Valentina," Scarlett said brightly. She closed her laptop as she stood from her chair. "It's been a while since we've hung out. I thought you forgot about me in the new semester."

"Nope."

Scarlett gave me a hug that I didn't return. She pulled back and rubbed my forearms. "So are you here for some art therapy?"

"I came to talk to you about something." I stepped out of her grasp and moved over to a workbench. She followed. "It's about the no phones or recording ban."

"What about it?" Scarlett sat on the stool opposite me. "Is it to sign a petition to get it revoked because you're not the first. I'm sorry to say Evergreen Academy is very much a dictatorship. The headmaster won't budge."

"It's about something I overheard. You know the Knights and how they have tortured me. This year I swore I would get back at them so I broke into the Knights' room and hid my phone to record them." I reached into my blazer and set the phone between us.

She clapped her hand over her mouth. "Valentina! Oh, I wish you hadn't told me that."

"Why?" I cocked my head. "I thought you were on my side?"

"I am, but if I'm ever questioned about this, I'll have to tell that you've been secretly recording the students."

"You wouldn't lie to protect me?"

"I'm sorry, no."

"That's okay. I wouldn't either." I tapped the phone awake. "That's why I have to share this."

"Share what? What did you re—?"

"—knows what she did to us."

"It's not right. She shouldn't be around kids. Scarlett LeBlanc is a predator."

"She's a pedophile, and she ruined our lives. If that wasn't bad enough, now we know she's a Spade."

"You think all the Spades are as twisted as her? Is that how they're chosen?"

"You have to be twisted to think of something like marks. What I really want to know is why Scarlett chose us to be the Knights?"

"It's just more of that pervert's sick games, Jaxson. She probably told herself she was doing something nice for her 'special little helpers.'"

Silence descended on the room after I closed the recording. I had watched Scarlett's face through the whole thing. The older woman cycled through surprise, anger, fear, and finally another emotion I couldn't place, but it shone clearly in her eyes as she looked at me.

She lifted a shaky finger at the phone. "None of that is true."

I slid off the stool. "That's for the police and the media to decide."

"Do not move!" She lashed out and slammed her hand on the bench next to us, blocking me in.

Stepping back, I kept my voice calm. "Relax, Scarlett. My bodyguard is right outside."

Scarlett's freckles were stark on her pale cheeks. "You can't show anyone that," she rasped. "It's all lies."

"Yeah, but you would say that, wouldn't you?"

She gaped at me. "You know me, Valentina!" Scarlett put her hand to her chest. "I've been a friend to you, and I've never once done anything inappropriate."

I shook the phone. "Isn't that because I'm too old for you?"

The injured act dropped for the barest of moments and a snarl curled her lips. "That is enough! Give me the phone!"

I leaped back just as she lunged. Her hand swiped empty air.

"One scream and Kane runs in gun waving." I moved to the other side of the work bench, keeping it between us. "I'm not giving you this phone."

"If you don't—"

"But I'll promise not to show it to anyone if you sign this." I took a single sheet of paper from my pocket and set it before her. "It's your resignation letter."

She swiped it off the desk in a single move. "I will not be blackmailed. You have made a serious mistake, Valentina. The headmaster will see you expelled for this and—"

"Ugh. Forget this. If you won't sign"—I pulled up the recording and hovered over the share button—"then I'm posting this on my page."

"No, stop!"

"Sign it." My voice was so cold it chilled me. "Now."

Scarlett fell off the stool to snatch the letter from the floor. I put the pen on the table before she was back.

The letter shook in her trembling hands as she read it. She spoke, but it wasn't the words on the paper.

"I am not a predator. I *loved* those boys. I was there for them when their parents weren't. Nannies and cooks and tutors and drivers filled their lives. They used their fortunes to make sure they'd never have to raise their kids. They could talk to me. They could—"

"So you admit it."

She turned furious eyes on me. "I did nothing wrong!"

"Just like you did nothing wrong when you marked me? Think carefully before you deny. Remember I was there in the woods and I still have your mask. All I have to do is take it to the other staff and prove it was you who wore it that night."

Scarlett's face morphed before my eyes. Gone was the puffy, snarling mess and out came a true mask. Her expression smoothed out until it was blank. "I don't know what you're talking about."

"They say it on the recording too. You're a Spade."

"That recording is nothing but malicious talk from unhappy students." Scarlett signed her name with a flourish. "But I will not allow it to ruin my reputation. Here." She flung the paper. It bounced off my left boob and sailed to the floor. "Now delete it. I want to see you do it."

I picked the letter up. "I never told you I would do that. What I'm actually going to do is hold on to this so that I don't meet with any more *accidents.* If another planter falls from the sky or flaming tape balls end up in my room, I send this wide."

I gave her my back and marched toward the door.

"If I am who you say I am..."

I stopped dead.

"A Spade." Scarlett's voice slithered into my ear. "Then do you honestly believe that the way you handled this was smart?"

I spoke without turning around. "I believe that you're a sick piece of shit who preys on innocent children. You have no idea the pain you've caused, or you don't care, either way... don't count on me to protect your secret. You'll never hurt another child again."

Crash!

I spun as her stool toppled over. Scarlett darted around the table, eyes flashing with cold fury. I quickly grabbed the knob. I cracked the door open and she staggered to a halt.

"I should have dropped another on your head and made damn sure," she hissed, not letting her voice carry to the bodyguard outside. "You're such a stupid little girl, Valentina. Don't know when to quit. When to *leave.*" Scarlett's whole body shook with the force of her pants. I saw the restraint in the coiled tightness of her limbs.

"If you wanted me gone so badly, why did you help me? Why be nice to me? Why tell me about Walter?"

She barked a laugh and it startled me worse than the malice in her eyes. "Walter? Oh please. Who cares about that useless idiot? It wasn't about him. It was *never* about him. And that people thought he was some kind of threat to the Spades is laughable. He was a jumped-up brat who didn't know his place... just like you."

Wasn't about him?

"If he didn't matter, why was he killed? Do you all just do this for fun? Is that what the Spades are really about?"

Scarlett rose to her full height. Her amusement fled in the face of an emotion I couldn't name. "The Spades keep things as they should be, and I will do the same as those who came before me and those who will come after."

"No, Scarlett." I place my hand over my chest and the button cam that hid beneath. "You're done." I lurched forward, pulling the door with me. "You should have made damn sure the first time. Now it's my turn."

I slammed the door hard enough to shake the lockers.

"Everything okay, Miss Moon?"

My heart rattled my ribcage like a convict trying to escape. It took a few seconds for me to answer him. "Fine, Kane. I'm going back to my room. I'm tired."

Together we left the main building and crossed the courtyard to my dorm.

"I'm staying in until dinner," I told him while putting my key in the lock. "So you can go."

"I will return at six. Call me if you need me to come sooner."

I said bye, stepped in, and waited five minutes before opening the door again. Having the no-phone ban not apply to me seemed nice until you remembered you couldn't call anyone but your bodyguard.

Luckily, the boys and I agreed to meet at the cliffs after my talk with Scarlett. I got her to say she attacked me and all but admit what she did to the boys. This was it for her. We had done it.

I hope they're there. And that I remember the way as well as I said I did.

The quad was full of people tossing the ball around or lazing in the afternoon sun, but none of them paid attention to me hurrying through. The woods beckoned me inside and surrounded me in their music. The leaves shook with the wind, rustling high above, while birds and critters added to the chorus. A snapped twig joined the noise and I peered over my shoulder.

Nothing. I should hurry up. They must be waiting.

I hurried through the trodden path until light shone up ahead. I rushed out into the clearing and saw...

...no one. The guys weren't here yet.

I glanced at the chairs.

I'll chill until they—

Loud footsteps sounded behind me, and before I could turn, I was hit hard.

I went down as a body collapsed on top of me. "Give me the phone!"

A hand pressed down on my skull, pushing me into the dirt, while the other scrabbled at my pockets.

"Valentina!"

A scream, and then the weight on me was gone. I wrenched my head up, gasping, and saw Ezra and Scarlett grappling in the dirt. I shakily got to my knees as she reeled back and punched him in the throat. Ezra's hand flew to his neck and she took the chance to buck him off.

Then she came for me.

"Give it to me!"

I tried to get away, but I stumbled and she fell on me again. Vicious hands tangled in my hair and I screamed as I was dragged. Dragged further from Ezra... and closer to the cliff.

"I loved those boys! I won't let you or the world turn it into something sordid! They needed me! Me!"

I pounded and clawed at the hands in my hair. "Let me go! Let go!"

"Valentina!"

Relief so strong it mingled with my tears of pain hit me when I saw Ryder, Jaxson, and Maverick burst through the trees. Ezra struggled to his feet, and the four of them ran at us, leaping on Scarlett a few feet from the edge.

I was wrestled from her grasp. Maverick pulled me into his arms and wrapped me to his chest while the others got off of her. They all came to my side as Scarlett rose. She was a terrifying sight to behold. Blood gushed from a cut on her forehead. The naked hate on her face made me press myself closer to Maverick.

"Give. Me. The. Phone," she snarled.

I broke—fear and pain surging through me as I yanked the phone out of my pocket. "If you want the fucking thing so bad then have it!"

I threw it. The phone crested high over our heads and Scarlett's head snapped back as she followed its flight. She jumped, straining to reach it, and... missed.

The phone soared over the edge of the cliff and Scarlett went with it. Her screams echoed through the clearing until I could hear them no more.

"No..." I broke free of Maverick's arms and rushed to the edge. Four hands stopped me.

"It wasn't your fault, Valentina." Jaxson drew me to him. He laced our hands together. "It was not your fault."

"No one will know about this." Maverick took the other hand—dwarfing my delicate fingers in his strong ones.

"You didn't do anything wrong." Ezra pressed himself to my back, banishing the chill that was taking hold of me. "We won't let anything happen to you."

Ryder stepped into my sight. The wind played with his raven locks but nothing could stop me from seeing his eyes. He brushed his fingers across my cheek.

"We'll protect you."

Bound

Five people bound by the most terrible secret... and something else.

I never thought I could forgive them. I didn't believe there was still a heart inside of me that could forgive. But my boys, my knights, were taking down my walls and claiming a piece for themselves.

All I wanted was to lock our secret away and enter junior year as though the past never happened...

...but someone won't let me.

Someone knows what we did and the price for their silence may be more than I can give.

The game will only grow more vicious until lines are drawn in the battle for who truly rules Evergreen Academy.

Mailing List

Join my mailing list for info about new releases and treats. No spam ever.

Mailing list: https://www.subscribepage.com/rubyvincent-page

ABOUT THE AUTHOR

Ruby Vincent is a published author with many novels under her belt but now she's taking a fun foray into contemporary romance. She loves saucy heroines, bold alpha males, and weaving a tale where both get their happy ever after.

Made in the USA
Coppell, TX
08 April 2021

53399439R00142